SOLDIERS THREE
AND OTHER STORIES

ART-TYPE EDITION

SOLDIERS THREE
AND OTHER STORIES
By RUDYARD KIPLING

THE WORLD'S
POPULAR CLASSICS

BOOKS, INC.
PUBLISHERS
NEW YORK   BOSTON

CONTENTS

Soldiers Three

PREFACE

THIS small book contains, for the most part, the further adventures of my esteemed friends and sometimes allies, Privates Mulvaney, Ortheris, and Learoyd, who have already been introduced to the public. Those anxious to know how the three most cruelly maltreated a member of Parliament; how Ortheris went mad for a space; how Mulvaney and some friends took the town of Lungtungpen; and how little Jhansi McKenna helped the regiment when it was smitten with cholera, must refer to a book called "Plain Tales from the Hills." I would have reprinted the four stories in this place, but Dinah Shadd says that "tearin' the tripes out av a book wid a pictur' on the back, all to make Terence proud past reasonin'," is wasteful, and Mulvaney himself says that he prefers to have his fame "dishpersed most notoriously in sev'ril volumes." I can only hope that his desire will be gratified.

RUDYARD KIPLING

THE SOLID MULDOON

Did you see John Malone, wid his shinin', brand-new hat?
Did ye see how he walked like a grand aristocrat?
There was flags an' banners wavin' high an' dhress and
    shtyle were shown,
But the best av all the company was Misther John Malone.
                    —John Malone.

THIS befell in the old days, and, as my friend Private Mulvaney was specially careful to make clear, the Unregenerate.

There had been a royal dog-fight in the ravine at the back of the rifle-butts, between Learoyd's Jock and Ortheris's Blue Rot—both mongrel Rampur hounds, chiefly ribs and teeth. It lasted for twenty happy, howling minutes, and then Blue Rot collapsed and Ortheris paid Learoyd three rupees, and we were all very thirsty. A dog-fight is a most heating entertainment, quite apart from the shouting, because Rampurs fight over a couple of acres of ground. Later, when the sound of belt-badges clinking against the necks of beer-bottles had died away, conversation drifted from dog to man fights of all kinds. Humans resemble red-deer in some respects. Any talk of fighting seems to wake up a sort of imp in their breasts, and they bell one to the other, exactly like challenging bucks. This is noticeable even in men who consider themselves superior to privates of the line; it shows the refining influence of civilization and the march of progress.

Tale provoked tale, and each tale more beer. Even dreamy Learoyd's eyes began to brighten, and he unburdened himself of a long history in which a trip to Malham Cove, a girl at Pately Brigg, a ganger, himself and a pair of clogs were mixed in drawling tangle.

"An' so Ah coot's yead oppen from t' chin to t' hair an' he was abed for t' matter o' a month," concluded Learoyd, pensively.

Mulvaney came out of a reverie—he was lying down—and flourished his heels in the air. "You're a man, Learoyd," said he, critically, "but you've only fought wid men, an' that's an ivry-day expayrience; but I've stud up to a ghost, an' that was not an ivry-day expayrience."

"No?" said Ortheris, throwing a cork at him. "You git up an' address the 'ouse—you an' yer expayriences. Is it a bigger one nor usual?"

"'Twas the livin' trut'!" answered Mulvaney, stretching out a huge arm and catching Ortheris by the collar. "Now where are ye, me son? Will ye take the wurrud av the Lorrd out av my mout another time?" He shook him to emphasize the question.

"No, somethin' else, though," said Ortheris, making a dash at Mulvaney's pipe, capturing it, and holding it at arm's-length; "I'll chuck it acrost the ditch if you don't let me go!"

"You maraudin' hathen!   'Tis the only cutty I iver loved.   Handle her tinder or I'll chuck you acrost the nullah.   If that poipe was bruk— Ah! Give her back to me, sorr!"

Ortheris had passed the treasure to my hand.   It was an absolutely perfect clay, as shiny as the black ball at pool.   I took it reverently, but I was firm.

"Will you tell us about the ghost-fight if I do?" I said.

"Is ut the shtory that's troublin' you?   Av course I will.   I mint to all along.   I was only gettin' at ut my own way, as Popp Doggle said when they found him thrying to ram a cartridge down the muzzle.   Orth'ris, fall away!"

He released the little Londoner, took back his pipe, filled it, and his eyes twinkled.   He has the most eloquent eyes of any one that I know.

"Did I iver tell you," he began, "that I was wanst the divil av a man?"

"You did," said Learoyd, with a childish gravity that made Ortheris yell with laughter, for Mulvaney was always impressing upon us his merits in the old days.

"Did I iver tell you," Mulvaney continued, calmly, "that I was wanst more av a divil than I am now?"

"Mer—ria!   You don't mean it?" said Ortheris.

"Whin I was corp'ril—I was rejuced aftherwards —but, as I say, whin I was corp'ril, I was a divil of a man."

He was silent for nearly a minute, while his mind rummaged among old memories and his eyes glowed. He bit upon the pipe-stem and charged into his tale.

"Eyah! They was great times. I'm ould now; me hide's wore off in patches; sinthry-go has disconceited me, an' I'm a married man tu. But I've had my day, I've had my day, an' nothin' can take away the taste av that! Oh, my time past, whin I put me fut through ivry livin' wan av the Tin Commandmints between revelly and lights out, blew the froth off a pewter, wiped me mustache wid the back av me hand, an' slept on ut all as quiet as a little child! But ut's over—ut's over, an' 'twill niver come back to me; not though I prayed for a week av Sundays. Was there any wan in the ould rig'mint to touch Corp'ril Terence Mulvaney whin that same was turned out for sedukshin? I niver met him. Ivry woman that was not a witch was worth the runnin' afther in those days, an' ivery man was my dearest frind or—I had stripped to him an' we knew which was the betther av the tu.

"Whin I was corp'ril I wud not ha' changed wid the colonel—no, nor yet the commander-in-chief. I wud be a sargint. There was nothin' I wud not be! Mother av Hivin, look at me! Fwhat am I now? But no matther! I must get to the other ghosts— not the wans in my ould head.

"We was quartered in a big cantonmint—'tis no manner av use namin' names, for ut might give the barricks disrepitation—an' I was the imperor av the earth to my own mind, an' wan or tu women thought the same. Small blame to thim. Afther we had lain there a year, Bragin, the color sargint av E Comp'ny, wint an' took a wife that was lady's-maid to some big lady in the station. She's dead now, is Annie Bragin—died in child-bed at Kirpa Tal, or ut may ha' been Almorah—seven—nine years gone, an' Bragin he married ag'in. But she was a pretty woman whin Bragin inthrojuced her to cantonmint society. She had eyes like the brown av a buttherfly's wing whin the sun catches ut, an' a waist no thicker than my arm, an' a little sof' button av a mouth I wid ha' gone through all Asia bristlin' wid bay'nits to get the kiss av. An' her hair was as long as the tail av the colonel's charger—forgive me mintionin' that blunderin' baste in the same mouthful with Annie Bragin—but 'twas all shpun gold, an' time was whin a lock av ut was more than di'monds to me. There was niver pretty woman yet, an' I've had thruck wid a few, cud open the door to Annie Bragin.

" 'Twas in the Carth'lic chapel I saw her first, me oi rolling round as usual to see fwhat was to be seen. 'You're too good for Bragin, my love,' thinks I to mesilf, 'but that's a mistake I can put straight, or my name is not Terence Mulvaney.'

"Now take my wurrd for ut, you Orth'ris there an' Learoyd, an' kape out av the married quarters

—as I did not. No good iver comes av ut, an' there's
always the chance av your bein' found wid your face
in the dirt, a long picket in the back av your head,
an' your hands playing the fifes on the tread av another man's doorstep. 'Twas thus we found O'Hara,
he that Rafferty killed six years gone, when he wint
to his death wid his hair oiled, whistlin' 'Billy
O'Rourke' betune his teeth. Kape out av the married quarters, I say, as I did not. 'Tis onwholesim,
'tis dangerous, an' 'tis ivrything else that's bad, but—
Oh, my sowl, 'tis swate while ut lasts!

"I was always hangin' about there whin I was off
duty an' Bragin wasn't, but niver a sweet word be-
yon' ordinar' did I get from Annie Bragin. ' 'Tis
the pervarsity av the sect,' sez I to mesilf, an' gave
my cap another cock on my head an' straightened my
back—'twas the back av a dhrum-major in those days
—an' wint off as tho' I did not care, wid all the
women in the married quarters laughin'. I was pershuaded—most bhoys are, I'm thinkin'—that no
woman born av woman cud stand against me av I hild
up me little finger. I had reason for thinkin' that way
—till I met Annie Bragin.

"Time an' ag'in whin I was blanhandherin' in the
dusk a man wud go past me as quiet as a cat. 'That's
quare,' thinks I, 'for I am, or I should be, the only
man in these parts. Now what divilment can Annie
be up to?' Thin I called myself a blayguard for
thinkin' such things; but I thought thim all the same.
An' that, mark you, is the way av a man.

"Wan evenin' I said: 'Mrs. Bragin, manin' no disrespect to you, who is that corp'ril man'—I had seen the stripes though I cud niver get sight av his face—'who is that corp'ril man that comes in always whin I'm goin' away?'

" 'Mother av God!' sez she, turnin' as white as my belt; 'have you seen him, too?'

"'Seen him!' sez I; 'av coorse I have. Did ye want me not to see him, for'—we were standin' talkin' in the dhark, outside the veranda av Bragin's quarters —'you'd betther tell me to shut me eyes. Onless I'm mistaken, he's come now.'

"An', sure enough, the corp'ril man was walkin' to us, hangin' his head down as though he was ashamed av himself.

"'Good-night, Mrs. Bragin,' sez I, very cool; ' 'tis not for me to interfere wid your *a-moors;* but you might manage these things wid more dacincy. I'm off to canteen,' I sez.

"I turned on my heel and wint away, swearin' I wud give that man a dhressin' that wud shtop him messin' about the married quarters for a month an' a week. I had not tuk ten paces before Annie Bragin was hangin' on to my arm, an' I cud feel that she was shakin' all over.

" 'Stay wid me, Mister Mulvaney,' sez she; 'you're flesh an' blood, at the least—are ye not?'

" 'I'm all that,' sez I, an' my anger wint away in a flash. 'Will I want to be asked twice, Annie?'

"Wid that I slipped my arm round her waist, for,

begad, I fancied she had surrindered at discretion, an' the honors av war were mine.

"'Fwhat nonsince is this?' sez she, dhrawin' herself up on the tips av her dear little toes. 'Wid the mother's milk not dhry on your impident mouth? Let go!' she sez.

"'Did ye not say just now that I was flesh and blood?' sez I. 'I have not changed since,' I sez; an' I kep' my arm where ut was.

"'Your arms to yoursilf!' sez she, an' her eyes sparkild.

"'Sure, 'tis only human nature,' sez I; an' I kep' my arm where ut was.

"'Nature or no nature,' sez she, 'you take your arm away or I'll tell Bragin, an' he'll alter the nature av your head. Fwhat d'you take me for?' she sez.

"'A woman,' sez I; 'the prettiest in barricks.'

"'A wife,' sez she; 'the straightest in cantonmints!'

"Wid that I dropped my arm, fell back tu paces, an' saluted, for I saw that she mint fwhat she said."

"Then you know something that some men would give a good deal to be certain of. How could you tell?" I demanded, in the interests of science.

"'Watch the hand,' said Mulvaney; 'av she shuts her hand tight, thumb down over the knuckle, take up your hat an' go. You'll only make a fool av yourself av you shtay. But av the hand lies opin on the lap, or av you see her thryin' to shut ut, an' she can't—go on! She's not past reasonin' wid.'

"Well, as I was sayin', I fell back, saluted, an' was goin' away.

" 'Shtay wid me,' she sez. 'Look! He's comin' again.'

"She pointed to the veranda, an' by the hoight av impart'nince, the corp'ril man was comin out av Bragin's quarters.

" 'He's done that these five evenin's past,' sez Annie Bragin. 'Oh, fwhat will I do?'

" 'He'll not du ut again,' sez I, for I was fightin' mad.

"Kape away from a man that has been a thrifle crossed in love till the fever's died down. He rages like a brute baste.

"I wint up to the man in the veranda, manin', as sure as I sit, to knock the life out av him. He slipped into the open. 'Fwhat are doin' philanderin' about here, ye scum av the gutter?' sez I, polite, to give him his warnin', for I wanted him ready.

"He niver lifted his head, but sez, all mournful an' melancolius, as if he thought I wud be sorry for him: 'I can't find her,' sez he.

" 'My troth,' sez I, 'you've lived too long—you an' your seekin's an' findin's in a dacint married woman's quarters! Hould up your head, ye frozen thief av Genesis,' sez I, 'an' you'll find all you want an' more!'

"But he niver hild up, an' I let go from the

shoulder to where the hair is short over the eyebrows.

"'That'll do your business,' sez I, but it nearly did mine instid. I put my body-weight behind the blow, but I hit nothing at all, an' near put my shoulder out. The corp'ril man was not there, an' Annie Bragin, who had been watchin' from the veranda, throws up her heels, an' carries on like a cock whin his neck's wrung by the dhrummer-bhoy. I wint back to her, for a livin' woman, an' a woman like Annie Bragin, is more than a p'rade-groun' full av ghosts. I'd never seen a woman faint before, an' I stud like a shtuck calf, askin' her whether she was dead, an' prayin' her for the love av me, an' the love of her husband, an' the love av the Virgin, to opin her blessed eyes again, an' callin' mesilf all the names undher the canopy av hivin for plaguin' her wid my miserable *a-moors* whin I ought to ha' stud betune her an' this corp'ril man that had lost the number av his mess.

"I misremember fwhat nonsince I said, but I was not so far gone that I cud not hear a fut on the dirt outside. 'Twas Bragin comin' in, an' by the same token Annie was comin' to. I jumped to the far end av the veranda an' looked as if butter wudn't melt in my mouth. But Mrs. Quinn, the quartermaster's wife that was, had tould Bragin about my hangin' round Annie.

"'I'm not pleased wid you, Mulvaney,' sez

Bragin, unbucklin' his sword, for he had been on duty.

" 'That's bad hearin',' I sez, an' I knew that the pickets were dhriven in. 'What for, sargint?' sez I.

" 'Come outside,' sez he, 'an' I'll show you why.'

" 'I'm willin',' I sez; 'but my stripes are none so ould that I can afford to lose thim. Tell me now, who do I go out wid?' sez I.

"He was a quick man an' a just, an' saw fwhat I wud be afther. 'Wid Mrs. Bragin's husband,' sez he. He might ha' known by me askin' that favor that I had done him no wrong.

"We wint to the back av the arsenal an' I stripped to him, an' for ten minutes 'twas all I cud do to prevent him killin' himself against my fistes. He was mad as a dumb dog—just frothing wid rage; but he had no chanst wid me in reach, or learnin', or anything else.

" 'Will ye hear reason?' sez I, whin his first wind was runnin' out.

" 'Not whoile I can see,' sez he. Wid that I gave him both, one after the other, smash through the low gyard that he'd been taught whin he was a boy, an' the eyebrow shut down on the cheek-bone like the wing av a sick crow.

" 'Will you hear reason now, ye brave man?' sez I.

" 'Not while I can speak,' sez he, staggerin' up blind as a stump. I was loath to do ut, but I wint round an' swung into the jaw side-on an' shifted ut a half pace to the lef'.

" 'Will ye hear reason now?' sez I; 'I can't keep my timper much longer, an' 'tis like I will hurt you.'

" 'Not whoile I can stand,' he mumbles out av one corner av his mouth. So I closed an' threw him—blind, dumb, an' sick, an' jammed the jaw straight.

" 'You're an ould fool, Mister Bragin,' sez I.

" 'You're a young thief,' sez he, 'an' you've bruk my heart, you an' Annie betune you!'

"Thin he began cryin' like a child as he lay. I was sorry as I had niver been before. 'Tis an awful thing to see a strong man cry.

" 'I'll swear on the cross!' sez I.

" 'I care for none av your oaths,' sez he.

" 'Come back to your quarters,' sez I, 'an' if you don't believe the livin' begad, you shall listen to the dead,' I sez.

"I hoisted him an' tuk him back to his quarters. 'Mrs. Bragin,' sez I, 'here's a man that you can cure quicker than me.'

" 'You've shamed me before my wife,' he whimpers.

" 'Have I so?' sez I. 'By the look on Mrs. Bragin's face I think I'm in for a dhressin'-down worse than I gave you.'

"An' I was! Annie Bragin was woild wid indigna-tion. There was not a name that a dacint woman cud use that was not given my way. I've had my colonel walk roun' me like a cooper roun' a cask for fifteen minutes in ord'ly-room bekase I wint into the corner shop an' unstrapped lewnatic, but all that I iver tuk from his rasp av a tongue was ginger-pop to fwhat Annie tould me. An' that, mark you, is the way av a woman.

"Whin ut was done for want av breath, an' Annie was bendin' over her husband, I sez: ' 'Tis all thrue, an' I'm a blayguard an' you're an honest woman; but will you tell him of wan service that I did you?'

"As I finished speakin' the corp'ril man came up to the veranda, an' Annie Bragin shquealed. The moon was up, an' we cud see his face.

" 'I can't find her,' sez the corp'ril man, an' wint out like the puff av a candle.

" 'Saints stand betune us an' evil!' sez Bragin, crossin' himself; 'that's Flahy as the Tyrone Rig'-mint.'

" 'Who was he?' I sez, 'for he has given me a dale of fightin' this day.'

"Bragin tould us that Flahy was a corp'ril who lost his wife av cholera in those quarters three years gone, an' wint mad, an' 'walked' afther they buried him, huntin' for her.

'Well,' sez I to Bragin, 'he's been hookin' out as purgathory to keep company wid Mrs. Bragin ivry evenin' for the last fortnight. You may tell Mrs. Quinn, wid my love, for I know that she's been talkin' to you, an' you've been listenin', that she ought to onderstand the differ 'twixt a man an' a ghost.

She's had three husband,' sez I, 'an' you've got a
wife too good for you. Instid av which you lave
her to be boddered by ghosts an'—an' all manner av
evil spirruts. I'll niver go talkin' in the way av
politeness to a man's wife again. Good-night to you
both,' sez I, an' wid that I wint away, havin' fought
wid woman, man, and divil all in the heart av an
hour. By the same token I gave Father Victor wan
rupee to say a mass for Flahy's soul, me havin' discommoded him by shtickin' my fist into his systim."

"Your ideas of politeness seem rather large, Mulvaney," I said.

"That's as you look at ut," said Mulvaney, calmly;
"Annie Bragin niver cared for me. For all that, I
did not want to leave anything behin' me that Bragin
could take hould av to be angry wid her about—
whin an honust wurrd cud ha' cleared all up. There's
nothing like opin-speakin'. Orth'ris, ye scut, let me
put me oi to that bottle, for my throat's as dhry as
whin I thought I wud get a kiss from Annie Bragin.
An' that's fourteen years gone! Eyah! Cork's own
city an' the blue sky above ut—an' the times that was
—the times that was!"

THE GOD FROM THE
MACHINE

THE GOD FROM THE MACHINE

HIT a man an' help a woman an' ye can't be far wrong any ways.—*Maxims of Private Mulvaney*.

THE Inexpressibles gave a ball. They borrowed a seven-pounder from the Gunners, and wreathed it with laurels, and made the dancing-floor plate-glass, and provided a supper, the like of which had never been eaten before, and set two sentries at the door of the room to hold the trays and program cards. My friend, Private Mulvaney, was one of the sentries, because he was the tallest man in the regiment. When the dance was fairly started the sentries were released, and Private Mulvaney fled to curry favor with the mess sergeant in charge of the supper. Whether the mess sergeant gave or Mulvaney took, I cannot say. All that I am certain of is that, at suppertime, I found Mulvaney with Private Ortheris, two-thirds of a ham, a loaf of bread, half a paté de foie gras, and two magnums of champagne, sitting on the roof of my carriage. As I came up I heard him saying:

"Praise be a danst doesn't come as often as ord'ly-room, or, by this an' that, Orth'ris, me son, I wud be the dishgrace av the rig'mint instid av the brightest jool in uts crown."

"*Hand* the colonel's pet noosince," said Ortheris, who was a Londoner. "But wot makes you curse your rations? This 'ere fizzy stuff's good enough."

"Stuff, ye oncivilized pagin! 'Tis champagne we're dhrinkin' now. 'Tisn't that I am set ag'in. 'Tis the quare stuff wid the little bits av black leather in it. I misdoubt I will be distressin'ly sick wid it in the mornin'. Fwhat is ut?"

"Goose liver," I said, climbing on the top of the carriage, for I knew that it was better to sit out with Mulvaney than to dance many dances.

"Goose liver, is ut?" said Mulvaney. "Faith, I'm thinkin' thim that makes it wud do betther to cut up the colonel. He carries a power av liver undher his right arrum whin the days are warm an' the nights chill. He wud give thim tons an' tons of liver. 'Tis he sez so. 'I'm all liver today,' sez he; an' wid that he ordhers me ten days C. B. for as moild a dhrink as iver a good sodger tuk betune his teeth."

"That was when 'e wanted for to wash 'isself in the fort ditch," Ortheris explained. "Said there was too much beer in the barrack water-butts for a God-fearing man. You was lucky in gittin' orf with wot you did, Mulvaney."

"You say so? Now I'm pershuaded I was cruel hard trated, seein' fwhat I've done for the likes av him in the days whin my eyes were wider opin than they are now. Man alive, for the colonel to whip me on the peg in that way! Me that have saved

the repitation av a ten times better man than him!
'Twas ne-farious, an' that manes a power av evil!"

"Never mind the nefariousness," I said. "Whose
reputation did you save?"

"More's the pity, 'twasn't my own, but I tuk more
trouble wid ut than av ut was. 'Twas just my way,
messin' wid fwhat was no business av mine. Hear
now!" He settled himself at ease on the top of the
carriage. "I'll tell you all about ut. Av coorse I
will name no names, for there's wan that's an orf-cer's
lady now, that was in ut, and no more will I name
places, for a man is thracked by a place."

"Eyah!" said Ortheris, lazily, "but this is a mixed
story wot's comin'."

"Wanst upon a time, as the childer-books say, I
was a recruity."

"Was you, though?" said Ortheris; "now that's
extryordinary!"

"Orth'ris," said Mulvaney, "av you opin thim lips
av your again, I will, savin' your presince, sorr, take
you by the slack av your trousers an' heave you."

"I'm mum," said Ortheris. "Wot 'appened when
you was a recruity?"

"I was a betther recruity than you iver was or will
be, but that's neither here nor there. Thin I became
a man, an' the divil of a man I was fifteen years
ago. They called me Buck Mulvaney in thim days,
an', begad, I tuk a woman's eye. I did that! Ortheris, ye scrub, fwhat are ye sniggerin' at? Do you
misdoubt me?"

"Devil a doubt!" said Ortheris; "but I've 'eard summat like that before."

Mulvaney dismissed the impertinence with a lofty wave of his hand and continued:

"An' the orf'cers av the rig'mint I was in in thim days was orf'cers—gran' men, wid a manner on 'em, an' a way wid 'em such as is not made these days—all but wan—wan o' the capt'ns. A bad dhrill, a wake voice, an' a limp leg—thim three things are the signs av a bad man. You bear that in your hid, Orth'ris, me son.

"An' the colonel av the rig'mint had a daughter—wan av thim lamb-like, bleatin', pick-me-up-an'-carry-me-or-I'll-die gurls such as was made for the natural prey av men like the capt'n who was iverlastin' payin' coort to her, though the colonel he said time an' over, 'Kape out av the brute's way, my dear.' But he niver had the heart for to send her away from the throuble, bein' as he was a widower, an' she their wan child."

"Stop a minute, Mulvaney," said I; "how in the world did you come to know these things?"

"How did I come?" said Mulvaney, with a scornful grunt; "bekase I'm turned durin' the quane's pleasure to a lump av wood, lookin' out straight forninst me, wid a—a—candelabbrum in my hand, for you to pick your cards out av, must I not see nor feel? Av coorse I du! Up my back, an' in my boots, an' in the short hair av the neck—that's where I kape my eyes whin I'm on duty an' the reg'lar wans

are fixed. Know! Take my word for it, sorr, ivrything an' a great dale more is known in a rig'mint;
or fwhat wud be the use av a mess sargint, or a sargint's wife doin' wet-nurse to the major's baby? To
reshume. He was a bad dhrill, was this capt'n—a
rotten bad dhrill—an' whin first I ran me eye over
him, I sez to myself: 'My militia bantam!' I sez,
'my cock of a Gosport dunghill'—'twas from Portsmouth he came to us—'there's combs to be cut,' sez I,
'an' by the grace av God, 'tis Terence Mulvaney
will cut thim.'

"So he wint menowderin', and minanderin', an'
blandandhering roun' an' about the colonel's daughter, a' she, poor innocint, lookin' at him like a com-
m'ssariat bullock looks at the comp'ny cook. He'd
a dhirty little scrub av a black mustache, an' he
twisted an' turned ivry wurrd he used as ave he found
ut too sweet for to spit out. Eyah! He was a
tricky man an' a liar by natur'. Some are born so.
He was wan. I knew he was over his belt in money
borrowed from natives; besides a lot av other mathers
which, in regard to your presince, sorr, I will oblitherate. A little av fwhat I knew, the colonel knew, for
he wud have none av him, an' that, I'm thinkin',
by fwhat happened aftherwards, the capt'n knew.

"Wan day, being mortial idle, or they wud never
ha' thried ut, the rig'mint gave amshure theatricals
—orf'cers an' orf'cers ladies. You've seen the likes
time an' again, sorr, an' poor fun 'tis for them that
sit in the back row an' stamp wid their boots for the

honor av the rig'mint. I was told off for to shif'
the scenes, haulin' up this an' draggin' down that.
Light work ut was, wid lashins av beer and the gurl
that dhressed the orf'cers ladies . . . but she died in
Aggra twelve years gone, an' my tongue's gettin' the
betther av me. They was actin' a play thing called
'Sweethearts,' which you may ha' heard av, an' the
colonel's daughter she was a lady's-maid. The capt'n
was a boy called Broom—Spread Broom was his name
in the play. Thin I saw—ut come out in the actin'—
fwhat I niver saw before, an' that was that he was no
gentleman. They was too much together, thim two,
a-whisperin' behind the scenes I shifted, an' some
av what they said I heard; for I was death—blue
death and ivy—on the comb-cuttin'. He was iverlastin'ly oppressing her to fall in wid some sneakin'
schame av his, an' she was thryin' to stand out against
him, but not as though she was set in her will. I
wonder now in thim days that my ears did not grow
a yard on me head wid list'nin'. But I looked straight
forninst me, an' hauled up this an' dragged down
that, such as was my duty, an' the orf'cers ladies sez
one to another, thinkin' I was out av listen-reach:
'Fwhat an obliging young man is this Corp'ril Mulvaney!' I was a corp'ril then. I was rejuced aftherwards, but, no matther, I was a corp'ril wanst.

"Well, this 'Sweethearts' business wint on like
most amshure theatricals, an' barrin' fwhat I suspicioned, 'twasn't till the dhress-rehearsal that I saw
for certain that thim two—he the blackguard, an' she

no wiser than she should ha' been—had put up an evasion."

"A what?"

"E-vasion! Fwhat you lorruds an' ladies call an elopement. E-vasion I calls it, bekaze, exceptin' whin 'tis right an' natural an' proper, 'tis wrong an' dhirty to steal a man's wan child not knowing her own mind. There was a sargint in the comm'ssariat who set my face upon e-vasions. I'll tell you about that—"

"Stick to the bloomin' captains, Mulvaney," said Ortheris; "comm'ssariat sargints is low."

Mulvaney accepted the emendations and went on:

"Now, I knew that the colonel was no fool, any more than me, for I was hild the smartest man in the rig'mint, an' the colonel was the best orf'cer commandin' in Asia; so fwhat he said an' I said was a mortial truth. We knew that the capt'n was bad, but, for reasons which I have already oblitherated, I knew more than me colonel. I wud ha' rolled out his face wid the butt av my gun before permittin' av him to steal the gurl. Saints knew av he wud ha' married her, and av he didn't she wud be in great tormint, an' the divil av what you, sorr, call a 'scandal.' But I niver shtruck, niver raised me hand on my shuperior orf'cer; an' that was a merricle now I come to considher it."

"Mulvaney, the dawn's risin'," said Ortheris, "an' we're no nearer 'ome than we was at the beginnin'. Lend me your pouch. Mine's all dust."

Mulvaney pitched his pouch across, and Ortheris filled his pipe afresh.

"So the dhress-rehearsals came to an end, an', becase I was curious, I stayed behind whin the scene-shiftin' was ended, an' I shud ha' been in barricks, lyin' as flat as a toad under a painted cottage thing. They was talkin' in whispers, an' she was shiverin' an' gaspin' like a fresh-hukked fish. 'Are you sure you've got the hang av the manewvers?' sez he, or wurrds to that effec', as the coortmartial sez. 'Sure as death,' sez she, 'but I misdoubt 'tis cruel hard on my father.' 'Damn your father,' sez he, or any ways 'twas fwhat he thought, 'the arrangement is as clear as mud. Jungi will drive the carri'ge afther all's over, an' you come to the station, cool an' aisy, in time for the two-o'clock thrain, where I'll be wid your kit.' 'Faith,' thinks I to myself, 'thin there's a ayah in the business tu!'

"A powerful bad thing is a ayah. Don't you niver have any thruck wid wan. Thin he began sootherin her, an' all the orf'cers an' orf'cers ladies left, an' they put out the lights. To explain the theory av the flight, as they sat at muskthry, you must under-stand that afther this 'Sweethearts'' nonsince was ended, there was another little bit av a play called 'Couples'—some kind av couple or another. The gurl was actin' in this, but not the man. I suspicioned he'd go to the station wid the gurl's kit at the end av the first piece. 'Twas the kit that flusthered me, for I knew for a capt'n to go trapesing about the impire

wid the Lord knew what av a *truso* on his arrum was
nefarious, an' wud be worse than easin' the flag, so
far as the talk aftherward wint."

" 'Old on, Mulvaney. Wot's *truso?*" said Ortheris.

"You're a oncivilized man, me son. Whin a gurl's
married, all her kit an' 'coutrements are *truso*, which
manes weddin'-portion. An' 'tis the same whin she's
running' away, even wid the biggest blackguard on
the arrmy list.

"So I made my plan av campaign. The colonel's
house was a good two miles away. 'Dennis,' sez I
to my color-sargint, 'av you love me lend me your
kyart, for me heart is bruk an' me feet is sore wid
trampin' to and from this foolishness at the Gaff.'
An' Dennis lent ut, wid a rampin', stampin' red stal-
lion in the shafts. Whin they was all settled down
to their 'Sweethearts' for the first scene, which was
a long wan, I slips outside and into the kyart. Mother
av Hivin! but I made that horse walk, an' we came
into the colonel's compound as the divil wint through
Athlone—in standin' leps. There was no one there
excipt the servints, an' I wint round to the back an'
found the girl's ayah.

" 'Ye black brazen Jezebel,' sez I, 'sellin' your
masther's honor for five rupees—pack up all the Miss
Sahib's kit an' look slippy! Capt'n Sahib's order,'
sez I; 'going to the station we are,' I sez, an' wid that
I laid my finger to my nose an' looked the schamin'
sinner I was.

" '*Bote acchy*,' says she; so I knew she was in the business, an' I piled up all the sweet talk I'd iver learned in the bazaars on to this she-bullock, an' prayed av her to put all the quick she knew into the thing. While she packed, I stud outside an' sweated, for I was wanted for to shif' the second scene. I tell you, a young gurl's e-vasion manes as much baggage as a rig'mint on the line av march! 'Sints help Dennes's springs,' thinks I, as I bundled the stuff into the thrap, 'for I'll have no mercy!'

" 'I'm comin' too,' says the ayah.

" 'No, you don't,' sez I, 'later—*pechy*! You *baito* where you are. I'll *pechy* come an' bring you *sart*, along with me, you mauridin' '—niver mind fwhat I called her.

"Thin I wint for the Gaff, an' by the special ordher av Providence, for I was doin' a good work you will ondershtand, Dennis's springs hild toight. 'Now, whin the capt'n goes for that kit,' thinks I, 'he'll be throubled.' At the end av 'Sweethearts' off the capt'n runs in his kyart to the colonel's house, an' I sits down on the steps and laughs. Wanst an' again I slipped in to see how the little piece was goin', an' whin ut was near endin' I stepped out all among the carriages an' sings out very softly, 'Jungi!' Wid that a carri'ge began to move, an' I waved to the dhriver. 'Hitherao!' sez I, an' he hitheraoed till I judged he was at a proper distance, an' thin I tuk him, fair an square betune the eyes, all I knew for good or bad, an' he dhropped wid a guggle like the canteen beer-

engine whin ut's runnin' low. Thin I ran to the
kyart an' tuk out all the kit an' piled it into the
carr'ige, the sweat runnin' down my face in dhrops.
'Go home,' sez I to the sais; 'you'll find a man close
here. Very sick he is. Take him away, an' av you
iver say wan wurrd about fwhat you've *dekkoed*, I'll
marrow you till your own wife won't *sumjao* who
you are!' Thin I heard the stampin' av feet at the
ind av the play, an' I ran in to let down the curtain.
Whin they all came out the gurl thried to hide herself behind wan av the pillars, an' sez 'Jungi' in a
voice that wudn't ha' scared a hare. I run over to
Jungi's carr'ige an' tuk up the lousy old horse-blanket
on the box, wrapped my head an' the rest av me in
ut, an' dhrove up to where she was.

"'Miss Sahib,' sez I; 'going to the station. Captain Sahib's order!' an' widout a sign she jumped in
all among her own kit.

"I laid to an' dhruv like steam to the colonel's
house before the colonel was there, an' she screamed
an' I thought she was goin' off. Out comes the ayah,
saying all sorts av things about the capt'n havin' come
for the kit an' gone to the station.

" 'Take out the luggage, you divil,' sez I, 'or I'll
murther you!'

"The lights av the thraps people comin' from the
Gaff was showin' acrost the parade-ground, an' by
this an' that, the way thim two women worked at
the bundles an' thrunks was a caution! I was dyin'
to help, but, seein' I didn't want to be known, I sat

wid the blanket roun' me an' coughed an' thanked the saints there was no moon that night.

"Whin all was in the house again, I niver asked for *bukshish* but dhruv tremenjus in the opp'site way from the other carr'ige an' put out my lights. Pres-intly, I saw a naygur man wallowin' in the road. I slipped down before I got to him, for I suspicioned Providence was wid me all through that night. 'Twas Jungi, his nose smashed in flat, all dumb sick as you please. Dennis's man must have tilted him out av the thrap. Whin he came to, 'Hutt!' sez I, but he began to howl.

" 'You black lump av dirt,' I sez, 'is this the way you dhrive your *gharri*? That *tikka* has been owin' an' fereowin' all over the bloomin' country this whole bloomin' night, an' you as *mut-walla* as Davey's sow. Get up, you hog!' sez I, louder, for I heard the wheels av a thrap in the dark; 'get up an' light your lamps, or you'll be run into!' This was on the road to the railway station.

" 'Fwhat the divil's this?' sez the capt'n's voice in the dhark, an' I could judge he was in a lather av rage.

" '*Gharri* dhriver here, dhrunk, sorr,' sez I; 'I've found his *gharri* sthrayin' about cantonmints, an' now I've found him.'

" 'Oh!' sez the capt'n; 'fwhat's his name?' I stooped down an' pretended to listen.

" 'He sez his name's Jungi, sorr,' sez I.

" 'Hould my harse,' sez the capt'n to his man, an'

wid that he gets down wid the whip an' lays into Jungi, just mad wid rage an' swearin' like the scut he was.

"I thought, afhter awhile, he wud kill the man, so I sez, 'Stop, sir, or you'll murdher him!' That dhrew all his fire on me, an' he cursed me into blazes, an' out again. I stud to attenshin an' saluted: 'Sorr,' sez I, 'av ivry man in this wurruld had his rights, I'm thinking that more than wan wud be beaten to a shakin's jelly for this night's work—that never came off at all, sorr, as you see?' 'Now,' thinks I to myself, 'Terence Mulvaney, you've cut your own throat, for he'll sthrike, an' you'll knock him down for the good av his sowl an' your own iverlastin' dishgrace!'

"But the capt'n never said a single wurrd. He choked where he stud, an' thin he wint into his thrap widout sayin' good-night, an' I went back to barricks."

"And then?" said Ortheris and I together.

"That was all," said Mulvaney; "niver another wurrd did I hear av the whole thing. All I know was that there was no e-vasion, an' that was fwhat I wanted. Now, I put ut to you, sorr, is ten days' C.B. a fit an' a proper tratement for a man who has behaved as me?"

"Well, any'ow," said Ortheris, "tweren't this 'ere colonel's daughter, an' you was blazin' copped when you tried to wash in the fort ditch."

"That," said Mulvaney, finishing the champage "is a shuparfluous an' impert'nint observation."

WITH THE MAIN GUARD

WITH THE MAIN GUARD

Der jungere Uhlanen
Sit round mit open mouth
While Breitmann tell dem stdories
Of fightin' in the South;
Und gif dem moral lessons,
How before der battle pops,
Take a little prayer to Himmel
Und a goot long drink of Schnapps.
    —*Hans Breitmann's Ballads.*

"Mary, Mother av Mercy, fwhat the divil possist us to take an' kape this malancolious counthry? Answer me that, Sorr."

It was Mulvaney who was speaking. The hour was one o'clock of a stifling hot June night, and the place was the main gate of Fort Amara, most desolate and least desirable of all fortresses in India. What I was doing there at that hour is a question which only concerns McGrath the Sergeant of the Guard, and the men on the gate.

"Slape," said Mulvaney, "is a shuparfluous necessity. This gyard'll shtay lively till relieved." He himself was stripped to the waist; Learoyd on the next bedstead was dripping from the skinful of water which Ortheris, arrayed only in white trousers, had just sluiced over his shoulders; and a fourth private was muttering uneasily as he dozed open-mouthed in the glare of the great guard-lantern. The heat under the bricked archway was terrifying.

"The worrst night that iver I remember. Eyah! Is all hell loose this tide?" said Mulvaney. A puff of burning wind lashed through the wicket-gate like a wave of the sea, and Ortheris swore.

"Are ye more heasy, Jock?" he said to Learoyd. "Put yer 'ead between your legs. It'll go orf in a minute."

"Ah don't care. Ah would not care, but ma heart is playin' tivvy-tivvy on ma ribs. Let me die! Oh, let me die!" groaned the huge Yorkshire man, who was feeling the heat acutely, being of fleshly build.

The sleeper under the lantern roused for a moment and raised himself on his elbow. "Die and be damned then!" he said. "I'm damned and I can't die!"

"Who's that?" I whispered, for the voice was new to me.

"Gentleman born," said Mulvaney; "Corp'ril wan year, sargint nex'. Red-hot on his c'mission, but dhrinks like a fish. He'll be gone before the cowld weather's here. So!"

He slipped his boot, and with the naked toe just touched the trigger of his Martini. Ortheris misunderstood the movement, and the next instant the Irishman's rifle was dashed aside, while Ortheris stood before him, his eyes blazing with reproof.

"You!" said Ortheris. "My Gawd, you! If it was you, wot would we do?"

"Kape quiet, little man," said Mulvaney, putting him aside, but very gently; " 'tis not me, nor will ut be me whoile Dinah Shadd's here. I was but showin' something."

Learoyd, bowed on his bedstead, groaned, and the gentleman ranker sighed in his sleep. Ortheris took Mulvaney's tendered pouch, and we three smoked gravely for a space while the dust-devils danced on the glacis and scoured the red-hot plain without.

"Pop?" said Ortheris, wiping his forehead.

"Don't tantalize wid talkin' av dhrink, or I'll sthuff you into your own breech-block an' fire you off!" grunted Mulvaney.

Ortheris chuckled, and from a niche in the veranda produced six bottles of gingerale.

"Where did ye get ut, ye Machiavel?" said Mulvaney. " 'Tis no bazaar pop."

" 'Ow do Hi know wot the orf'cers drink?" answered Ortheris. "Arst the mess-man."

"Ye'll have a disthrict coort-martial settin' on ye yet, me son," said Mulvaney, "but"—he opened a bottle—"I will not report ye this time. Fwhat's in the mess-kit is mint for the belly, as they say, 'specially whin that mate is dhrink. Here's luck! A bloody war or a—no, we've got the sickly season. War, thin!"—he waved the innocent "pop" to the four quarters of heaven. "Bloody war! North, east, south, an' west! Jock, ye quakin' hayrick, come an' dhrink."

But Learoyd, half mad with the fear of death presaged in the swelling veins of his neck, was imploring his Maker to strike him dead, and fighting for more air between his prayers. A second time Ortheris drenched the quivering body with water, and the giant revived.

"An' Ah divn't see thot a mon is i' fettle for gooin' on to live; an' Ah divn't see thot there is owt for t' livin' for. Hear now, lads! Ah'm tired—tired. There's nob-but watter i' ma bones. Let me die!"

The hollow of the arch gave back Learoyd's broken whisper in a bass boom. Mulvaney looked at me hopelessly, but I remembered how the madness of despair had once fallen upon Ortheris, that weary, weary afternoon on the banks of the Khemi River, and how it had been exorcised by the skillful magician Mulvaney.

"Talk, Terence!" I said, "or we shall have Learoyd slinging loose, and he'll be worse than Ortheris was. Talk! He'll answer to your voice."

Almost before Ortheris had deftly thrown all the rifles of the guard on Mulvaney's bedstead, the Irishman's voice was uplifted as that of one in the middle of a story, and turning to me, he said:

"In barricks or out of it, as you say, sorr, an Oirish rig'mint is the divil an' more. 'Tis only fit for a young man wid eddicated fisteses. Oh, the crame av disruption is an Oirish rig'mint, an' rippin', tear-

in', ragin' scattherers in the field av war! My first
rig'mint was Oirish—Faynians an' rebils to the heart
av their marrow was they, an' so they fought for the
widdy betther than most, bein' contrary—Oirish.
They was the Black Tyrone. You've heard av thim,
sorr?"

Heard of them! I knew the Black Tyrone for
the choicest collection of unmitigated blackguards,
dog-stealers, robbers of hen-roosts, assaulters of innocent citizens, and recklessly daring heroes in the
Army List. Half Europe and half Asia has had
cause to know the Black Tyrone—good luck be
with their tattered colors as glory has ever been!

"They was hot pickils an' ginger! I cut a man's
head tu deep wid my belt in the days av my
youth, an' afther some circumstances which I will
oblitherate, I came to the ould rig'mint, bearin' the
character av a man wid hands an' feet. But, as I
was goin' to tell you, I fell acrost the Black Tyrone
ag'in wan day whin we wanted thim powerful bad.
Orth'ris, me son, fwhat was the name av that place
where they sint wan comp'ny av us an' wan av the
Tyrone roun' a hill an' down again, all for to tache
the Paythans something they'd niver learned before?
After Ghuzni 'twas."

"Don't know what the bloomin' Paythans called
it. We called it Silver's Theayter. You know that,
sure!"

"Silver's Theater—so 'twas. A gut betune two
hill, as black as a bucket, an' as thin as a gurl's

waist. There was over-many Paythans for our convaynience in the gut, an' begad they called thimselves a reserve—bein' impident by natur! Our Scotchies an' lashins av Gurkys was poundin' into some Paythan rig'mints, I think 'twas. Scotchies an' Gurkys are twins bekaze they're so onlike, an' they get dhrunk together whin God plazes. Well, as I was sayin', they sint wan comp'ny av the Ould and wan av the Tyrone to double up the hill an' clane out the Paythan reserve. Orf'cers was scarce in thim days, fwhat wid dysintry an' not takin' care av thimselves, an' we was sint out wid only wan orf'cer for the comp'ny; but he was a man that had his feet beneath him, an' all his teeth in their sockuts."

"Who was he?" I asked.

"Captain O'Neil—Old Crook—Cruik-na-bullen —him that I tould ye that tale av whin he was in Burmah. Hah! He was a man. The Tyrone tuk a little orf'cer bhoy, but divil a bit was he in command, as I'll dimonstrate presintly. We an' they came over the brow av the hill, wan on each side av the gut, an' there was that ondacint reserve waitin' down below like rats in a pit.

" 'Howld on, men,' sez Crook, who tuk a mother's care av us always. 'Rowl some rocks on thim by way av visitin'-kyards.' We hadn't rowled more than twinty bowlders, an' the Paythans was beginnin' to swear tremenjus, whin the little orf'cer bhoy av the Tyrone shqueaks out acrost the valley: 'Fwhat the divil an' all are you doin', shpoilin' the fun for my men. Do you not see they'll stand?'

" 'Faith, that's a rare pluckt wan!' sez Crook. 'Niver mind the rocks, men. Come along down an' take tay wid thim!'

" 'There's damned little sugar in ut!' sez my rear-rank man; but Crook heard.

" 'Have ye not all got spoons?' he sez, laughin', an' down we wint as fast as we cud. Learoyd bein' sick at the base, he, av coorse, was not there."

"Thot's a lie!" said Learoyd, dragging his bedstead nearer. "Ah gotten *thot* theer, an' you knaw it, Mulvaney." He threw up his arms, and from the right armpit ran, diagonally through the fell of his chest, a thin white line terminating near the fourth left rib.

"My mind's goin'," said Mulvaney, the unabashed. "Ye were there. Fwhat was I thinkin' of? 'Twas another man, av coorse. Well, you'll remimber thin, Jock, how we an' the Tyrone met wid a bang at the bottom an' got jammed past all movin' among the Paythans."

"Ow! It wos a tight 'ole. Hi was squeeged till I thought I'd blommin' well bust," said Artheris, rubbing his stomach meditatively.

" 'Twas no place for a little man, but wan little man"—Mulvaney put his hand on Ortheris's shoulder—"saved the life av me. There we shtuck, for divil a bit did the Paythans flinch, an' divil a bit dare we; our business bein' to clear 'em out. An'

the most exthryordinar' thing av all was that we an'
they jus rushed into each other's arrums, an' there
was no firing for a long time. Nothin' but knife
an' bay'nit when we cud get our hands free; that
was not often. We was breast on to thim, an' the
Tyrone was yelpin' behind av us in a way I didn't
see the lean av at first. But I knew later, an' so did
the Paythans.

" 'Knee to knee!' sings out Crook, wid a laugh
whin the rush av our comin' into the gut shtopped,
an' he was huggin' a hairy great Paythan, neither
bein' able to do anything to the other, tho' both was
wishful.

" 'Breast to breast!' he says, as the Tyrone was
pushin' us forward closer an' closer.

" 'And hand over back!' sez a sargint that was
behin'. I saw a sword lick out past Crook's ear like
a snake's tongue, an' the Paythan was tuk in the
apple av his throat like a pig at Dromeen fair.

" 'Thank ye, Brother Inner Guard,' sez Crook,
cool as a cucumber widout salt. 'I wanted that
room.' An' he wint forward by the thickness av a
man's body, having turned the Paythan undher him.
The man bit the heel off Crook's boot in his death-
bite.

" 'Push, men!' sez Crook. 'Push, ye paper-backed
beggars!' he sez. 'Am I to pull ye through?' So
we pushed, an' we kicked, an' we swung, an' we
swore, an' the grass bein' slippery, our heels wouldn't

bite, an' God help the frontrank man that wint down that day!"

" 'Ave you ever bin in the pit hentrance o' the Vic. on a thick night?" interrupted Ortheris. "It was worse nor that, for they was goin' one way, and we wouldn't 'ave it. Leastway, Hi 'adn't much to say."

"Faith, me son, ye said ut, thin. I kep' the little man betune my knees as long as I cud, but he was pokin' roun' wid his bay'nit, blindin' an' stiffin' feroshus. The devil of a man is Orth'ris in a ruction—aren't ye?" said Mulvaney.

"Don't make game!" said the cockney. "I knowed I wasn't no good then, but I guv 'em compot from the lef' flank when we opened out. No!" he said, bringing down his hand with a thump on the bedstead, "a bay'nit ain't no good to a little man—might as well 'ave a bloomin' fishin'-rod! I 'ate a clawin', maulin' mess, but gimme a breech that's wore out a bit, an' hamminition one year in store, to let the powder kiss the bullet, an' put me somewheres where I ain't trod on by 'ulkin' swine like you, an' s'elp me Gawd, I could bowl you over five times outer seven at height 'undred. Would yer try, you lumberin' Hirishman?"

"No, ye wasp. I've seen ye do ut. I say there's nothin' better than the bay'nit, wid a long reach, a double twist ave ye can, an' a slow recover."

"Dom the bay'nit," said Learoyd, who had been

listening intently. "Look-a-here!" He picked up
a rifle an inch below the foresight with an under-
handed action, and used it exactly as a man would
use a dagger.

"Sitha," said he, softly, "thot's better than owt,
for a man can bash t' face wi' thot, an', if he divn't,
he can break t' forearm o' t' gaard. 'Tis not i' t'
books, though. Gie me t' butt."

"Each does ut his own way, like makin' love,"
said Mulvaney, quietly; "the butt or the bay'nit or
the bullet accordin' to the natur' av the man. Well,
as I was sayin', we shtuck there breathin' in each
other's faces an' swearin' powerful, Orth'ris cursin'
the mother that bore him bekase he was not three
inches taller.

"Prisintly he sez: 'Duck, ye lump, an I can get
a man over your shouldher!'

"'You'll blow me head off,' I sez, throwin' my
arm clear; 'go through under my armpit, ye blood-
thirsty little scut,' sez I, 'but don't shtick me or I'll
wring your ears round.'

"Fwhat was ut ye gave the Paythan man forninst me, him that cut at me whin I cudn't move hand
or foot? Hot or cowld, was ut?"

"Cold," said Ortheris, "up an' under the rib-jint.
'E come down flat. Best for you 'e did."

"Thrue, my son! This jam thing that I'm talkin' about lasted for five minutes good, an' thin we
got our arms clear an' wint in. I misremimber
exactly fwhat I did, but I didn't want Dinah to be

a widdy at the Depot. Thin, after some promish-
kuous hackin' we shtuck again, an' the Tyrone behin'
was callin' us dogs an' cowards an' all manners av
names; we barrin' their way.

" 'Fwhat ails the Tyrone?' thinks I; 'they're the
makin's av a most convanient fight here.'

"A man behind me sez beseechful an' in a whisper:
'Let me get at thim! For the love av Mary give me
room beside ye, ye tall man!'

" 'An' who are you that's so anxious to be kilt?'
sez I, widout turnin' my head, for the long knives
was dancin' in front like the sun on Donegal Bay
whin ut's rough.

" 'We've seen our dead,' he sez, squeezin' into
me; 'our dead that was men two day gone! An'
me that was his cousin by blood could not bring Tim
Coulan off! Let me get on,' he sez, 'let me get to
thim or I'll run ye through the back!'

" 'My troth,' thinks I, 'if the Tyrone have seen
their dead, God help the Paythans this day!' An'
thin I knew why the Oirish was ragin' behind us as
they was.

"I gave room to the man, and he ran forward wid
the Haymakers' Lift on his bay'nit an' swung a Paythan clear off his feet by the belly-band av the brute,
an' the iron bruk at the lockin'-ring.

" 'Tim Coulan'll slape aisy to-night,' sez he wid
a grin; an' the next minut his head was in two halves
and he wint down grinnin' by sections.

"The Tyrone was pushin' an' pushin' in, an' our

men was swearin' at thim, an' Crook was workin'
away in front av us all, his sword-arm swingin' like
a pump-handle an' his revolver spittin' like a cat.
But the strange thing av ut was the quiet that lay
upon. 'Twas like a fight in a drame—except for
thim that was dead.

"Whin I gave room to the Orishman I was expinded an' forlorn in my inside. 'Tis a way I have,
savin' your prisince, sorr, in action. 'Let me out,
bhoys,' sez I, backin' in among thim. 'I'm goin' to
be onwell!' Faith they gave me room at the wurrud,
though they would not ha' given room for all hell
wid the chill off. When I got clear, I was, savin'
your presince, sorr, outragis sick bekaze I had dhrunk
heavy that day.

"Well an' far out av harm was a sargint av the
Tyrone sittin' on the little orf'cer bhoy who had
stopped Crook from rowlin' the rocks. Oh, he was
a beautiful bhoy, an' the long black curses was sliding
out av his innocint mouth like mornin'-jew from a
rose!

"'Fwhat have you got there?' sez I to the sargint.

"'Wan av her majesty's bantams wid his spurs
up,' sez he. 'He's goin' to coort-martial me.'

"'Let me go!' sez the little orf'cer bhoy. 'Let me
go and command my men!' mainin' thereby the Black
Tyrone, which was beyond any command—ay, even
av they had made the divil a field-orf'cer.

"'His father howlds my mother's cowfeed in

Clonmel,' sez the man that was sittin' on him. 'Will I go back to his mother an' tell her that I've let him throw himself away? Lie still, ye little pinch av dynamite, an' coort-martial me afterwards.'

"'Good,' sez I; ''tis the likes av him makes the likes av the commandher-in-chief, but we must presarve thim. Fwhat d' you want to do, sorr?' sez I, very politeful.

"'Kill the beggars—kill the beggars!' he shqueaks; his big blue eyes fairly brimmin' wid tears.

"'An' how'll ye do that?' sez I. 'You've shquibbed off your revolver like a child wid a cracker; you can make no play wid that fine large sword av yours; an' your hand's shakin' like an asp on a leaf. Lie still and grow,' sez I.

"'Get back to your comp'ny,' sez he; 'you're insolint!'

"'All in good time,' sez I, 'but I'll have a dhrink first.'

"Just thin Crook comes up, blue an' white all over where he wasn't red.

"'Wather!' sez he; 'I'm dead wid drouth! Oh, but it's a gran' day!'

"He dhrank half a skinful, and the rest he tilts into his chest, an' it fair hissed on the hairy hide av him. He sees the little orf'cer boy undher the sargint.

"'Fwhat's yonder?' sez he.

"'Mutiny, sorr,' sez the sargint, an' the orf'cer

bhoy begins pleadin' pitiful to Crook to be let go; but divil a bit wud Crook budge.

" 'Kape him there,' he sez, ' 'tis no child's work this day. By the same token,' sez he, 'I'll confishcate that iligant nickel-plated scent-sprinkler av yours, for my own has been vomitin' dishgraceful!'

"The fork ov his hand was black wid the backspit av the machine. So he tuk the orf'cer bhoy's revolver. Ye may, look, sorr, but, by my faith, there's a dale more done in the field than iver gets into field ordhers!

" 'Come on, Mulvaney,' sez Crook; 'is this a coort-martial?' The two av us wint back together into the mess an' the Paythans were still standin' up. They was not too impart'nint though, for the Tyrone was callin' wan to another to remember Tim Coulan.

"Crook stopped outside av the strife an' looked anxious, his eyes rowlin' roun'.

" 'Fwhat is ut, sorr?' sez I; 'can I get ye anything?'

" 'Where's a bugler?" sez he.

"I wint into the crowd—our men was drawhin' breath behin' the Tyrone, who was fightin' like sowls in tormint—an' prisintly I come acrost little Frehan, our bugler bhoy, pokin' roun' among the best wid a rifle an' bay'nit.

" 'Is amusin' yourself fwhat you're paid for, ye limb?' sez I, catchin' him by the scruff. 'Come out av that an' attind to your duty,' I sez; but the bhoy was not pleased.

" 'I've got wan,' sez he, grinnin', 'big as you, Mulvaney, an' fair half as ugly. Let me go get another.'

"I was dishpleased at the personality av that remark, so I tucks him under my arm an' carries him to Crook, who was watchin' how the fight wint. Crook cuffs him till the bhoy cries, an' thin sez nothin' for a whoile.

"The Paythans began to flicker onaisy, an' our men roared. 'Open ordher! Double!' sez Crook. 'Blow, child, blow for the honor av the British arrmy!'

"That bhoy blew like a typhoon, an' the Tyrone an' we opined out as the Paythan's broke, an' I saw the fwhat had gone before wud be kissin' an huggin' to fwhat was to come. We'd dhruv thim into a broad part av the gut whin they gave, an' thin we opined out an' fair danced down the valley, dhrivin' thim before us. Oh, 'twas lovely, an' stiddy, too! There was the sargints on the flanks av what was left av us, kapin' touch, an' the fire was runnin' from flank to flank, an' the Paythans was dhroppin'. We opined out wid the widenin' av the valley, an' whin the valley narrowed we closed again like the sthicks on a lady's fan, an' at the bar ind av the gut where they thried to stand, we fair blew them off their feet, for we had expinded very little ammunition by reason av the knife work."

"Hi used thirty rounds goin' down that valley," said Ortheris, "an' it was gentleman's work. Might 'a' done it in a white 'andkerchief an' pink silk stockin's, that part. Hi was on in that piece."

"You could ha' heard the Tyrone yellin' a mile away," said Mulvaney, "an' 'twas all their sargints cud do to get them off. They was mad—mad—mad! Crook sits down in the quiet that fell whin he had gone down the valley, an' covers his face wid his hands. Prisintly we all came back again accordin' to our natures and disposishuns, for they, mark you, show through the hide av a man in that hour.

"'Bhoys! bhoys!' sez Crook to himself 'I misdoubt we could ha' engaged at long range an' saved betther men than me.' He looked at our dead an' said no more.

"'Captain dear,' sez a man av the Tyrone comin' up wid his mouth bigger than iver his mother kissed ut, spittin' blood like a whale; 'captain dear,' sez he, 'if wan or two in the sthalls have been discommoded, the gallery have enjoyed the performinces av a Roshus.'

"Thin I knew that man for the Dublin dock-rat he was—wan av the bhoys that made the lessee av Silver's Theater gray before his time wid tearin' out the bowils av the benches an' t'rowin' thim into the pit. So I passed the wurrud that I knew when I was in the Tyrone, an' we lay in Dublin. 'I don't know

who 'twas,' I whispers, 'an' I don't care, but any ways
I'll knock the face av you, Tim Kelley.'

" 'Eyah!' sez the man, 'was you there, too? We'll
call ut Silver's Theater.' Half the Tyrone, knowin'
the ould place, tuk ut up: so we called ut Silver's
Theater.

"The little orf'cer bhoy av the Tyrone was thrim-
blin' an' cryin'. He had no heart for the coort-
martials that he talked so big upon. 'Ye'll do well
later,' sez Crook, very quiet, 'for not bein' allowed
to kill yourself for amusement.'

" 'I'm a disgraced man!' sez the little orf'cer
bhoy.

" 'Put me undher arrest, sorr, if you will, but,
by my sowl, I'd do ut again sooner than face your
mother wid you dead,' sez the sargint that had sat
on his head, standin' to attention an' salutin'. But
the young wan only cried as tho' his little heart was
breakin'.

"Thin another man av the Tyrone came up, wid
the fog av fightin' on him."

"The what, Mulvaney?"

"Fog av fightin'. You know, sorr, that, like
makin' love, ut takes each man diff'rint. Now, I
can't help bein' powerful sick whin I'm in action.
Orth'ris, here, niver stops swearin' from ind to ind,
an' the only time that Learoyd opins his mouth to
sing is whin he is messin' wid other people's heads;
for he's a dhirty fighter is Jock Learoyd. Recruities

sometime cry, an' sometime they don't know fwhat they do, an' sometime they are all for cuttin' throats, an' such like dirtiness; but some men get heavy-dead dhrunk on the fightin'. This man was. He was staggerin', an' his eyes were half shut, an' we cud hear him dhraw breath twinty yards away. He sees the little orf'cer bhoy, an' comes up, talkin' thick an' drowsy to himsilf. 'Blood the young whelp!' he sez; 'blood the young whelp'; an' wid that he threw up his arms, shpun roun', an' dropped at our feet, dead as a Paythan, an' there was niver sign or scratch on him. They said 'twas his heart was rotten, but oh, 'twas a quare thing to see!

"Thin we wint to bury our dead, for we wud not lave them to the Paythans, an' in movin' among the haythen we nearly lost that little orf'cer bhoy. He was for givin' wan divil wather and layin' him aisy against a rock. 'Be careful, sorr,' sez I; 'a wounded Paythan's worse than a live wan.' My troth, before the words was out of my mouth, the man on the ground fires at the orf'cer bhoy lanin' over him, an' I saw the helmit fly. I dropped the butt on the face av the man an tuk his pistol. The little orf'cer boy turned very white, for the hair av half his head was singed away.

" 'I tould you so, sorr!' sez I; an' afther that, whin he wanted to help a Paythan I stud wid the muzzle contagious to the ear. They dare not do anythin' but curse. The Tyrone was growlin' like dogs over a bone that has been taken away too soon, for they had seen their dead an' they wanted to kill ivery sowl on the ground. Crook tould thim that he'd blow the hide off any man that misconducted himself; but, seeing that ut was the first time the Tyrone had iver seen their dead, I do not wondher they were on the sharp. 'Tis a shameful sight! Whin I first saw ut I wud niver ha' given quarter to any man north of the Khaibar—no, nor woman neither, for the women used to come out afther dhark—*Auggrh!*

"Well, evenshually we buried our dead an' tuk away our wounded, an' come over the brow av the hills to see the Scotchies an' the Gurkys taking tay with the Paythans in bucketsfuls. We were a gang av dissolute ruffians, for the blood had caked the dust, an' the sweat had cut the cake, an' our baynits was hangin' like butcher's steels one way or another.

"A staff orf'cer man, clean as a new rifle, rides up an' sez: 'What damned scarecrows are you?'

" 'A company av her majesty's Black Tyrone, an' wan av the ould rig'mint,' sez Crook very quiet, givin' our visitors the flure as 'twas.

" 'Oh!' sez the staff orf'cer; 'did you dislodge that reserve?'

" 'No!' sez Crook, an' the Tyrone laughed.

" 'Thin fwhat the divil have ye done?'

" 'Desthroyed ut,' sez Crook, an' he took us on, but not before Toomey that was in the Tyrone sez aloud, his voice somewhere in his stummick: 'Fwhat in the name av misfortune does this parrit widout a tail mane by shtoppin' the road av his betthers?'

"The staff orf'cer wint blue, and Toomey makes him pink by changin' to the voice av a minow-derin' woman an' sayin': 'Come an' kiss me, major dear, for me husband's at the wars an' I'm all alone at the depot.'

"The staff orf'cer wint away, an' I cud see Crook's shouldhers shakin'.

"His corp'ril checks Toomey. 'Lave me alone,' sez Toomey, widout a wink. 'I was his batman be-fore he was married an' he knows fwhat I mane, av you don't. There's nothin' like livin' in the hoight av society.' D'you remimber that, Orth'ris!"

"Hi do, Toomey, 'e died in 'orspital, next week it was, 'cause I bought 'arf his kit; an' I remember after that—"

"GUARRD, TURN OUT!"

The relief had come; it was four o'clock. "I'll catch a kyart for you, sorr," said Mulvaney, diving hastily into his accouterments. "Come up to the top av the fort an' we'll pershue our invistigations into McGrath's shtable." The relieved guard stroll-ed round the main bastion on its way to the swim-ming-bath, and Learoyd grew almost talkative. Ortheris looked into the fort ditch and across the plain. "Ho! it's weary waitin' for Ma-ary!" he hummed; "but I'd like to kill some more bloomin' Paythans before my time's up. War! Bloody war! North, east, south, and west."

"Amen," said Learoyd, slowly.

"Fwhat's here?" said Mulvaney, checking at a

blur of white by the foot of the old sentry box. He stopped and touched it. "It's Norah—Norah Mc-Taggart! Why, Nonie darlin' fwhat are ye doin' out av your mother's bed at this time?"

The two-year-old child of Sergeant McTaggart must have wandered for a breath of cool air to the very verge of the parapet of the fort ditch. Her tiny night-shift was gathered into a wisp round her neck and she moaned in her sleep. "See there!" said Mulvaney; "poor lamb! Look at the heat-rash on the innocint skin av her. 'Tis hard—crool hard even for us. Fwhat must it be for these? Wake up, Nonie, your mother will be woild about you. Begad, the child might ha' fallen into the ditch!"

He picked her up in the growing light, and set her on his shoulder, and her fair curls touched the grizzled stubble of his temples. Ortheris and Lea-royd followed snapping their fingers, while Norah smiled at them a sleepy smile. Then caroled Mul-vaney, clear as a lark, dancing the baby on his arm:

> "If any young man should marry you,
>   Say nothin' about the joke;
> That iver ye slep' in a sinthry box,
>   Wrapped up in a soldier's cloak.

"Though, on my soul, Nonie," he said, gravely, "there was not much cloak about you. Niver mind, you won't dhress like this ten years to come. Kiss your friends an' run along to your mother."

Nonie, set down close to the married quarters,

nodded with a quiet obedience of the soldier's child, but, ere she pattered off over the flagged path, held up her lips to be kissed by the three musketeers. Ortheris wiped his mouth with the back of his hand and swore sentimentally; Learoyd turned pink; and the two walked away together. The Yorkshireman lifted up his voice and gave in thunder the chorus of "The Sentry Box," while Ortheris piped at his side.

" 'Bin to a bloomin' sing-song, you two?" said the artilleryman, who was taking his cartridge down to the Morning Gun. "You're overmerry for these dashed days."

> "I bid ye take care o' the brat, said he,
> For it comes of a noble race,"

bellowed Learoyd. The voices died out in the swimming-bath.

"Oh, Terrence!" I said, dropping into Mulvaney's speech, when we were alone, "it's you that have the tongue!"

He looked at me wearily; his eyes were sunk in his head, and his face was drawn and white. "Eyah!" said he; "I've blandandhered thim through the night somehow, but can thim that helps others help themselves? Answer me that, sorr!"

And over the bastions of Fort Amara broke the pitiless day.

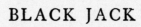

BLACK JACK

BLACK JACK

To the wake av Tim O'Hara
Came company,
All St. Patrick's Alley
Was there to see.
—*The Wake of Tim O'Hara.*

THERE is a writer called Mr. Robert Louis Stevenson, who makes most delicate inlay-work in black and white, and files out to the fraction of a hair. He has written a story about a suicide club, wherein men gambled for death, because other amusements did not bite sufficiently. My friend Private Mulvaney knows nothing about Mr. Stevenson, but he once assisted informally at a meeting of almost such a club as that gentleman has described; and his words are true.

As the Three Musketeers share their silver, tobacco, and liquor together, as they protect each other in barracks or camp, and as they rejoice together over the joy of one, so do they divide their sorrows. When Ortheris's irrepressible tongue has brought him into cells for a season, or Learoyd has run amuck through his kit and accouterments, or Mulvaney has indulged in strong waters, and under their influence reproved his commanding officer, you can see the trouble in the faces of the untouched twain. And the rest of the regiment know that comment or jest is unsafe. Generally the three avoid orderly-room and the corner shop that follows, leaving both to the young bloods who have not sown their wild oats; but there are occasions. . . . For instance, Ortheris was sitting on the draw-bridge of the main gate of Fort Amara, with his hands in his pockets and his pipe, bowl down, in his mouth. Learoyd was lying at full length on the turf of the glacis, kicking his heels in the air, and I came round the corner and asked for Mulvaney.

Ortheris spat in the ditch and shook his head. "No good seein' 'im now," said Ortheris; " 'e's a bloomin' camel. Listen."

I heard on the flags of the veranda opposite to the cells, which are close to the guard-room, a measured step that I could have identified in the tramp of an army. There were twenty paces *crescendo*, a pause, and then twenty *diminuendo*.

"That's 'im," said Ortheris; "my Gawd, that's 'im! All for a bloomin' button you could see your face in an' a bit o' lip that a bloomin' hark-angel would 'a' guv back."

Mulvaney was doing pack-drill—was compelled, that is to say, to walk up and down for certain hours in full marching order, with rifle, bayonet, ammunition, knapsack, and overcoat. And his offense was being dirty on parade! I nearly fell into the fort ditch with astonishment and wrath, for Mulvaney is the smartest man that ever mounted guard, and would as soon think of turning out uncleanly as of dispensing with his trousers.

"Who was the sergeant that checked him?" I asked.

"Mullins, o' course," said Ortheris. "There ain't no other man would whip 'im on the peg so. But Mullins ain't a man. 'E's a dirty little pig-scraper, that's wot 'e is."

"What did Mulvaney say? He's not the kind of man to take that quietly."

"Said! Bin better for 'im if 'e'd shut 'is mouth. Lord, 'ow we laughed! 'Sargint,' 'e sez, 'ye say I'm dirty. Well,' sez he, 'when your wife lets you blow your own nose for yourself, perhaps you'll know wot dirt is. You're himperfectly eddicated, sargint,' sez 'e, an' then we fell in. But after p'rade, 'e was up an' Mullins was swearin' 'imself black in the face at ord'ly-room that Mulvaney 'ad called 'im a swine an' Lord knows wot all. You know Mullins. 'E'll 'ave 'is 'ead broke in one o' these days. 'E's too big a bloomin' liar for ord'nary consumption. 'Three hours can an' kit,' sez the colonel; 'not for bein' dirty on p'rade, but for 'avin' said somethin' to Mullins, tho' I do not believe,' sez 'e, 'you said wot 'e said you said.' You know 'e never speaks to the colonel for fear o' gettin' 'imself fresh cropped."

Mullins, a very young and very much married sergeant, whose manners were partly the result of

innate depravity and partly of imperfectly digested
board school, came over the bridge, and most rudely
asked Ortheris what he was doing.

"Me?" said Ortheris. "Ow! I'm waiting for
my c'mission. 'Seed it comin' along yit?'"

Mullins turned purple and passed on. There was
the sound of a gentle chuckle from the glacis where
Learoyd lay.

"'E expects to get his c'mission some day," ex-
claimed Ortheris; "Gawd 'elp the mess that 'ave to
put their 'ands into the same kiddy as 'im! Wot
time d'you make it, sir? Fower! Mulvaney'll be
out in 'arf an hour. You don't want to buy a dorg,
sir, do you? A pup you can trust—'arf Rampore by
the colonel's gray'ound."

"Ortheris," I answered, sternly, for I knew what
was in his mind, "do you mean to say that—"

"I didn't mean to arx money o' you, any'ow,"
said Ortheris; "I'd 'a' sold you the dorg good an'
cheap, but—but—I know Mulvaney'll want somethin' after we've walked 'im orf, an' I ain't got nothin' nor 'e 'asn't neither. I'd sooner sell you the
dorg, sir. 'S trewth I would!"

A shadow fell on the draw-bridge, and Ortheris
began to rise into the air, lifted by a huge hand upon
his collar.

"Onything but t' braass," said Learoyd, quietly,
as he held the Londoner over the ditch. "Onything but t' braass, Orth'ris ma son! Ah've got
one rupee eight annas of ma own." He showed

two coins, and replaced Ortheris on the draw-bridge rail.

"Very good," I said; "where are you going to?"

"Goin' to walk 'im orf wen 'e comes out—two miles or three or fower," said Ortheris.

The footsteps within ceased. I heard the dull thud of a knapsack falling on a bedstead, followed by the rattle of arms. Ten minutes later Mulvaney, faultlessly attired, his lips compressed and his face as black as a thunder-storm, stalked into the sunshine on the draw-bridge. Learoyd and Ortheris sprung from my side and closed in upon him, both leaning toward as horses lean upon the pole. In an instant they had disappeared down the sunken road to the cantonments, and I was left alone. Mulvaney had not seen fit to recognize me; wherefore, I felt that his trouble must be heavy upon him.

I climbed one of the bastions and watched the figures of the Three Musketeers grow smaller and smaller across the plain. They were walking as fast as they could put foot to the ground, and their heads were bowed. They fetched a great compass round the parade-ground, skirted the cavalry lines, and vanished in the belt of trees that fringes the low land by the river.

I followed slowly and sighted them—dusty, sweating, but still keeping up their long, swinging tramp—on the river-bank. They crashed through the forest reserve, headed toward the bridge of boats, and presently established themselves on the bow of one of the pontoons. I rode cautiously till I saw three puffs of white smoke rise and die out in the clear evening air, and knew that peace had come again. At the bridge-head they waved me forward with gestures of welcome.

"Tie up your 'orse," shouted Ortheris, "an' come on, sir. We're all goin' 'ome in this 'ere bloomin' boat."

From the bridge-head to the forest officers' bunga-low is but a step. The mess-man was there, and would see that a man held my horse. Did the sahiib require aught else—a peg, or beer? Ritchie Sahib had left half a dozen bottles of the latter, but since the sahib was a friend of Ritchie Sahib, and he, the mess-man, was a poor man—

I gave my order quietly, and returned to the bridge. Mulvaney had taken off his boots, and was dabbling his toes in the water; Learoyd was lying on his back on the pontoon; and Ortheris was pretend-ing to row with a big bamboo.

"I'm an ould fool," said Mulvaney, reflectively, "dhraggin' you two out here bekaze I was undher the black dog—sulkin' like a child. Me that was soldierin' when Mullins, an' be damned to him, was shquealin' on a counterpin for foive shillin's a week, an' that not paid! Bhoys, I've took you foive miles out av natural pevarsity. Phew!"

"Wot's the odds as long as you're 'appy?" said

Ortheris, applying himself afresh to the Bamboo. "As well 'ere as anywhere else."

Learoyd held up a rupee and an eight anna bit, and shook his head sorrowfully. "Five miles from t' canteen, all along o' Mulvaney's blasted pride."

"I know ut," said Mulvaney, penitently. "Why will ye come wid me? An' yet I wud be mortial sorry if ye did not—any time—though I am ould enough to know better. But I will do penance. I will take a dhrink av wather."

Ortheris squeaked shrilly. The butler of the forest bungalow was standing near the railings with a basket, uncertain how to clamber down to the pontoon.

"Might 'a' know'd you'd 'a' got liquor out o' bloomin' desert, sir," said Ortheris, gracefully, to me. Then to the mess-man: "Easy with them there bottles. They're worth their weight in gold. Jock, ye long-armed beggar, get out o' that an' hike 'em down."

Learoyd had the basket on the pontoon in an instant, and the Three Musketeers gathered round it with dry lips. They drank my health in due and ancient form, and thereafter tobacco tasted sweeter than ever. They absorbed all the beer, and disposed themselves in picturesque attitudes to admire the setting sun—no man speaking for awhile.

Mulvaney's head dropped upon his chest, and we thought that he was asleep.

"What on earth did you come so far for?" I whispered to Ortheris.

"To walk 'im 'orf, o' course. When 'e's been checked we allus walks 'im orf. 'E ain't fit to be spoke to those times—nor 'e ain't fit to leave alone neither. So we takes 'im till 'e is."

Mulvaney raised his head, and stared straight into the sunset. "I had my rifle," said he, dreamily, "an' I had my bay'nit, an' Mullins came round the corner, an' he looked in my face an' grinned dishpiteful. 'You can't blow your own nose,' sez he. Now, I can not tell fwhat Mullins's expayrience may ha' been, but Mother av God, he was nearer to his death that minut' than I have iver been to mine— and that's less than the thicknuss av a hair!"

"Yes," said Ortheris, calmly, "you'd look fine with all your buttons took orf, an' the band in front o' you, walkin' roun' slow time. We're both front rank men, me an' Jock, when the rig'ment's in hollow square. Bloomin' fine you'd look. 'The Lord giveth an' the Lord taketh awai—Heasy with that there drop! Blessed be the naime of the Lord!'" He gulped in a quaint and suggestive fashion.

"Mullins! Wot's Mullins?" said Learoyd, slowly. "Ah'd take a comp'ny o' Mullinses—ma hand behind me. Sitha, Mulvaney, dunnat be a fool."

"You were not checked for fwhat you did not do, an' made a mock av afther. 'Twas for less than that the Tyrone wud ha' sent O'Hara to hell, instid av lettin' him go by his own choosin', whin Rafferty shot him," retorted Mulvaney.

"And who stopped the Tyrone from doing it?" I asked.

"That ould fool who's sorry he didn't stick the pig Mullins." His head dropped again. When he raised it he shivered and put his hand on the shoulders of his two companions.

"Ye've walked the divil out av me, bhoys," said he.

Ortheris shot out the red-hot dottel of his pipe on the back of the hairy fist. "They say 'ell's 'otter than that," said he, as Mulvaney swore aloud. "You be warned so. Look yonder!"—he pointed across the river to a ruined temple—"Me an' you an' 'im"—he indicated me by a jerk of his head—"was there one day when Hi made a bloomin' show o' myself. You an' 'im stopped me doin' such—an' Hi was on'y wishful for to desert. You are makin' a bigger bloomin' show o' yourself now."

"Don't mind him, Mulvaney," I said; "Dinah Shadd won't let you hang yourself yet awhile, and you don't intend to try it either. Let's hear about the Tyrone and O'Hara. Rafferty shot him for fooling with his wife. What happened before that?"

"There's no fool like an ould fool. You know you can do anythin' wid me whin I'm talkin'. Did I say I wud like to cut Mullins' liver out? I deny the imputashin, for fear that Orth'ris here wud report me—Ah! You wud tip me into the

river, wud you? Sit quiet, little man. Any ways,
Mullins is not worth the trouble av an extry p'rade,
an' I will trate him wid outragis contimpt. The
Tyrone an' O'Hara! O'Hara an' the Tyrone, begad! Ould days are hard to bring back into the
mouth, but they're always inside the head."

Followed a long pause.

"O'Hara was a divil. Though I saved him, for
the honor av the rig'mint, from his death that time,
I say it now. He was a divil—a long, bould, black-
haired divil."

"Which way?" asked Ortheris.

"Women."

"Then I know another."

"Not more than in reason, if you name me, ye
warped walkin'-shtick. I have been young, an' for
why should I not have tuk what I could? Did I
iver, whin I was corp'ril, use the rise av my rank—
wan step an' that taken away, more's the sorrow
an' the fault av me!—to prosecute a nefarious
inthrigue, as O'Hara did? Did I, whin I was cor-
p'ril, lay my spite upon a man an' make his life a
dog's life from day to day? Did I lie, as O'Hara
lied, till the young wans in the Tyrone turned white
wid the fear av the judgment av God killin' them
all in a lump, as ut killed the women at Devizes?
I did not! I have sinned my sins an' I have made
my confesshin' an' Father Victor knows the worst
av me. O'Hara was tuk, before he cud spake, on

Rafferty's door-step, an' no man knows the worst av him. But this much I know!

"The Tyrone was recruited any fashion in the ould days. A draf' from Connemara—a draf' from Portsmouth—a draf' from Kerry, an' that was a blazin' bad draf'—here, there and iverywhere—but the large av thim was Oirish—Black Oirish. Now there are Oirish an' Oirish. The good are good as the best, but the bad are wurrst than the wurrst. 'Tis this way. They clog together in pieces as fast as thieves, an' no wan knows fwhat they will do till wan turns informer an' the gang is bruk. But ut begins again, a day later, meetin' in holes an' corners an' swearin' bloody oaths an' shtickin' a man in the back an' runnin' away, an' thin waitin' for the blood-money on the reward papers—to see if it's worth enough. Those are the Black Oirish, an' 'tis they that bring dishgrace upon the name av Oirland, an' thim I wud kill—as I nearly killed wan wanst.

"But to reshume. My room—'twas before I was married—was wid twelve av the scum av the earth—the pickin's av the gutter—mane men that wud neither laugh nor talk nor yet get dhrunk as a man shud. They thried some av their dog's thricks on me, but I dhrew a line round my cot, an' the man that thransgressed ut wint into hospital for three days good.

"O'Hara had put his spite on the room—he was

my color sargint—an' nothin' cud we do to plaze him. I was younger than I am now, an' I tuk what I got in the way av dressing down and punishmint-dhrill wid my tongue in my cheek. But it was diff'rint wid the others, an' why I can not say, excipt that some men are borrun mane an' go to dhirty murdher wher a fist is more than enough. Afther a whoile they changed their chune to me an' was desp'rit frien'ly—all twelve av thim cursin' O'Hara in chorus.

" 'Eyah,' sez I, 'O'Hara's a divil and I'm not for denyin' ut, but is he the only man in the worruld? Let him go. He'll get tired av findin' our kit foul an' our 'couterments onproperly kep'.'

" 'We will not let him go,' sez they.

" 'Thin take him,' sez I, 'an' a dashed poor yield you will get for your throuble.'

" 'Is he not misconductin' himself wid Slimmy's wife?" sez another.

" 'She's common to the rig'mint,' sez I. 'Fwhat has made ye this partic'lar on a suddint?'

" 'Has he not put his spite on the roomful av us? Can we do anythin' that he will not check for us?' sez another.

" 'That's thrue,' sez I.

" 'Will ye not help us to do aught,' sez another—'a big bould man like you?"

" 'I will break his head upon his shouldhers av he puts hand on me,' sez I. 'I will give him the lie av he says that I'm dhirty, an' I wud not mind duckin' him in the artillery troughs if ut was not that I'm thryin' for my shtripes.'

" 'Is that all ye will do?' sez another. 'Have ye no more spunk than that, ye blood-dhrawn——'

" 'Blood-dhrawn I may be,' says I, gettin' back to my cot an' makin' my line round ut; 'but ye know that the man who comes acrost this mark will be more blood-dhrawn than me. No man gives me the name in my mouth,' I sez. 'Ondersthand, I will have no part wid you in anythin' ye do, nor will I raise my fist to my shuperior. Is any wan comin' on?' sez I.

"They made no move, tho' I gave thim full time, but stud growlin' an' snarlin' together at wan ind av the room. I tuck up my cap and wint out to canteen, thinkin' no little av mesilf, an' there I grew most ondacintly dhrunk in my legs. My head was all reasonable.

" 'Houligan,' I sez to a man in E Comp'ny that was by way av bein' a friend av mine: 'I'm overtuk from the belt down. Do you give me the touch av your shouldher to presarve my formation an' march me acrost the ground into the high grass. I'll sleep ut off there,' sez I; an' Houligan—he's dead now, but good he was while he lasted—walked wid me, givin' me the touch whin I wint wide, ontil we came to the high grass, an', my faith, the sky, an' the earth was fair rowlin' undher me. I made for where the grass was thickust, an' there I slep off my liquor wid an aisy conscience. I did not desire

to come on books too frequint; my characther havin'
been shpotless for the good half av a year.

"Whin I roused, the dhrink was dyin' out in
me, an' I felt as though a she-cat had littered in my
mouth. I had not learned to hold my liquor wid
comfort in thim days. 'Tis little betther I am now.
'I will get Houligan to pour a bucket over my head,'
thinks I, an' wud ha' risen, but I heard some wan
say: 'Mulvaney can take the blame av ut for the
backslidin' hound he is.'

" 'Oho!' sez I, an' my head rang like a guard-
room gong; 'fwhat is the blame that this young man
must take to oblige Tim Vulmea?' For 'twas Tim
Vulmea that shpoke. I turned on my belly an'
crawled through the grass, a bit at a time, to where
the spache came from. There was the twelve av
my room sittin' down in a little patch, the dhry
grass wavin' above their heads an' the sin av black
murdher in their hearts. I put the stuff aside to get
clear view.

" 'Fwhat's that?' sez wan man, jumpin' up.

" 'A dog,' says Vulmea. 'You're a nice hand to
this job! As I said, Mulvaney will take the blame
—av ut comes to a pinch.'

" ' 'Tis harrd to swear a man's life away,' sez a
young wan.

" 'Thank ye for that,' thinks I. 'Now, fwhat the
divil are you paragins conthrivin' against me?'

" ' 'Tis as easy as dhrinkin' your quart,' sez Vulmea. 'At seven or thereon, O'Hara will come acrost

to the married quarters, goin' to call on Slimmy's
wife, the swine!   Wan av us'll pass the wurrd to the
room an' we shtart the divil an' all av a shine—
laughin' an' crackin' on an' t'rowin' our boots about.
Thin O'Hara will come to give us the ordher to
be quiet, the more by token bekaze the room-lamp
will be knocked over in the larkin'. He will take the
straight road to the ind door where there's the lamp
in the veranda, an' that'll bring him clear against the
light as he sthands. He will not be able to look
into the dhark. Wan av us will loose off, an' a
close shot ut will be, an' shame to the man that
misses. 'Twill be Mulvaney's rifle, she that is at
the head av the rack—there's no mistakin' that long-
shtocked, cross-eyed bitch even in the dhark.'

"The thief misnamed my ould firin'-piece out of
jealousy—I was pershuaded av that—an' ut made
me more angry than all.

"But Vulmea goes on: 'O'Hara will dhrop, an'
by the time the light's lit again, there'll be some
six av us on the chest av Mulvaney, cryin' murdher
an' rape. Mulvaney's cot is near the ind door, an'
the shmokin' rifle will be lyin' undher him whin
we've knocked him over. We know, an' all the
rig'mint knows, that Mulvaney has given O'Hara
more lip than any man av us. Will there be any
doubt at the coort-martial? Wud twelve honust
sodger-bhoys swear away the life av a dear, quiet,
swate-tempered man such as is Mulvaney—wid his
line av pipe-clay roun' his cot, threatenin' us wid

murdher av we overshtepped ut, as we can truthful testify?'

" 'Mary, Mother av Mercy!' thinks I to mysilf; 'it is this to have an unruly mimber an' fistes fit to use! Oh, the sneakin' hounds!'

"The big dhrops ran down my face, for I was wake wid the liquor an' had not the full av my wits about me. I laid shtill and heard thim workin' themselves up to swear my life by tellin' tales av ivry time I had put my mark on wan or another; an' my faith, they was few that was not so distinguished. 'Twas all in the way av fair fight, though, for niver did I raise my hand excipt whin they had provoked me to ut.

" ' 'Tis all well,' sez wan av thim, 'but who's to do this shootin'?'

" 'Fwhat matther?' sez Vulmea. ' 'Tis Mulvaney will do that—at the coort-martial.'

" 'He will so,' sez the man, 'but whose hand is put to the trigger—in the room?'

" 'Who'll do ut?' sez Vulmea, lookin' round, but divil a man answered. They began to dishpute till Kiss, that was always playin' Shpoil Five, sez: 'Thry the kyards!' Wid that he opined his jackut an' tuk out the greasy palamers, an' they all fell in wid the notion.

" 'Deal on!' sez Vulmea, wid a big rattlin' oath, 'an' the Black Curse av Shielygh come to the man that will not do his duty as the kyards say. Amin!'

" 'Black Jack is the masther,' says Kiss, dealin'.

Black Jack, sorr, I shud expaytiate to you, is the ace
of shpades which from time immemorial has been
intimately connected wid battle, murdher an' sudden
death.

"Wanst Kiss dealt an' there was no sign, but the
men was whoite wid the workin's av their sowls.
Twice Kiss dealt, an' there was a gray shine on their
cheeks like the mess av an egg. Three times Kiss
dealt an' they was blue. 'Have ye not lost him?'
sez Vulmea, wipin' the sweat on him. 'Let's ha'
done quick!' 'Quick ut is,' sez Kiss t'rowin' him
the kyard; an' ut fell face up on his knee—Black
Jack!

"Thin they all cackled wid laughin'. 'Duty thripp-
pence,' sez wan av thim, 'an' damned cheap at that
price!' But I cud see they all dhrew a little away
from Vulmea an' lef' him sittin' playin' wid the
kyard. Vulmea sez no word for awhoile but licked
his lips—cat-ways. Thin he threw up his head an'
made the men swear by ivry oath known an' unknown
to stand by him not alone in the room but at the
coort-martial that was to set on me! He tould off
five av the biggest to stretch me on my cot whin the
shot was fired, an' another man he tould off to put
out the light, an' yet another to load my rifle. He
wud not do that himself; an' that was quare, for
'twas but a little thing.

" 'Thin they swore over again that they wud not
bethray wan another, an' crep' out av the grass in
diff'rint ways, two by two. A mercy ut was that they

did not come on me. I was sick wid fear in the pit
av my stummick—sick, sick, sick! Afther they was
all gone, I wint back to the canteen an' called for a
quart to put a thought in me. Vulmea was there,
dhrinkin' heavy, an' politeful to me beyond reason.
'Fwhat will I do—fwhat will I do?' thinks I to mesilf whin Vulmea wint away.

"Prisintly the arm'rer sargint comes in stiffin' an'
crackin' on, not pleased wid any wan, bekaze the
Martini-Henri bein' new to the rig'mint in those
days we used to play the mischief wid her arrangements. 'Twas a long time before I cud get out av
the way av thryin' to pull back the back-sight an'
turnin' her over afther firin'—as if she was a Snider.

" 'Fwhat tailor-men do they give me to work wid?'
sez the arm'rer sargint. 'Here's Hogan, his nose
flat as a table, laid by for a week, an' ivry comp'ny
sendin' their arrums in knocked to small shivreens.'

" 'Fwhat's wrong wid Hogan, sargint?' sez I.

" 'Wrong!' sez the arm'rer sargint; 'I showed
him, as though I had been his mother, the way av
shtrippin' a 'Tini, and he shtrup her clane an' aisy. I
towld him to put her to again an' fire a blank into the
blow-pit to show how the dirt hung on the groovin'.
He did that, but he did not put in the pin av the
fallin'-block, an' av coorse whin he fired he was strook
by the block jumpin' clear. Well for him 'twas but
a blank—a full charge wud ha' cut his oi out.'

"I looked a trifle wiser than a boiled sheep's head.
'How's that sargint?' sez I.

" 'This way, ye blundherin' man, an' don't be doin' ut,' sez he. Wid that he shows me a Waster action—the breech av her all cut away to show the inside—an' so plazed was he to grumble that he dimonstrated fwhat Hogan had done twice over. 'An' that comes av not knowin' the wepping you're purvided wid,' sez he.

" 'Thank ye, sargint,' sez I; 'I will come to you again for further information.'

" 'Ye will not,' sez he. 'Kape your clanin'-rod away from the breech-pin or you will get into throuble.'

"I wint outside an' I could ha' danced wid delight for the grandeur av ut. 'They will load my rifle, good luck to thim, whoile I'm away,' thinks I, and back I wint to the canteen to give them their clear chanst.

"The canteen was fillin' wid men at the ind av the day. I made feign to be far gone in dhrink, an', wan by wan, all my roomful came in wid Vulmea. I wint away, walkin' thick and heavy, but not so thick an' heavy that any wan cud ha' tuk me. Sure and thrue, there was a kyartidge gone from my pouch an' lyin' snug in my rifle. I was hot wid rage against thim all, and I worried the bullet out wid my teeth as fast as I cud, the room bein' empty. Then I tuk my boot an' the clanin'-rod and knocked out the pin av the fallin'-block. Oh, 'twas music when that pin rowled on the flure! I put ut into my pouch an' stuck a dab av dirt on the holes in the plate, puttin' the fallin'-block back. 'That'll do your business, Vulmea,' sez I, lyin' easy on the cot. 'Come an' sit on my chest the whole room av you, an' I will take you to my bosom for the biggest divils that iver cheated halter.' I wud have no mercy on Vulmea. His oi or his life—little I cared!

"At dusk they came back, the twelve av thim, an' they had all been dhrinkin'. I was shammin' sleep on the cot. Wan man wint outside on the veranda. Whin he whistled they began to rage roun' the room an' carry on tremenjus. But I niver want to hear men laugh as they did—skylarkin' too! 'Twas like made jackals.

" 'Shtop that blasted noise!' sez O'Hara in the dark, an' pop goes the room lamp. I cud hear O'Hara runnin' up an' the rattlin' av my rifle in the rack an' the men breathin' heavy as they stud roun' my cot. I cud see O'Hara in the light av the veranda lamp, an' thin I heard the crack av my rifle. She cried loud, poor darlint, bein' mishandled. Next minut five men were holdin' me down. 'Go easy,' I sez; 'fwhat's ut all about?'

"Thin Vulmea, on the flure, raised a howl you cud hear from wan ind av cantonmints to the other. 'I'm dead, I'm butchered, I'm blind!' sez he. 'Saints have mercy on my sinful sowl! Sind for Father Constant! Oh, sind for Father Constant an' let me go clean!' By that I knew he was not so dead as I cud ha' wished.

"O'Hara picks up the lamp in the veranda wid a

hand as stiddy as a rest. 'Fwhat damned dog's thrick is this av yours?' sez he, and turns the light on Tim Vulmea that was shwimmin' in blood from top to toe. The fallin'-block had sprung free behin' a full charge av powther—good care I tuk to bite down the brass afther takin' out the bullet that there might be somethin' to give ut full worth—an' had cut Tim from the lip to the corner av the right eye, lavin' the eyelid in tatthers, an' so up an' along by the forehead to the hair. 'Twas more av a rakin' plow, if you will ondherstand, than a clean cut; an' niver did I see a man bleed as Vulmea did. The dhrink an' the stew that he was in pumped the blood strong. The minut the men sittin' on my chest heard O'Hara spakin' they scatthered each wan to his cot, an' cried out very politeful: 'Fwhat is ut, sargint?'

" 'Fwhat is ut!' sez O'Hara, shakin' Tim. 'Well an' good do you know fwhat ut is, ye skulkin' ditch-lurkin' dogs! Get a doolie, an' take this whimperin' scut away. There will be more heard av ut than any av you will care for.'

"Vulmea sat up rockin' his head in his hand an' moanin' for Father Constant.

" 'Be done!' sez O'Hara, dhraggin' him up by the hair. 'You're none so dead that you can not go fifteen years for thryin' to shoot me.'

" 'I did not,' sez Vulmea; 'I was shootin' me-silf.'

" 'That's quare,' sez O'Hara, 'for the front av my jackut is black wid your powther.' He tuk up

the rifle that was still warm an' began to laugh.
'I'll make your life hell to you,' sez he, 'for at-
tempted murdher an' kapin' your rifle onproperly.
You'll be hanged first an' thin put undher stoppages for four fifteen. The rifle's done for,' sez
he.

" 'Why, 'tis my rifle!' sez I, comin' up to look;
'Vulmea, ye divil, fwhat were you doin' wid her
—answer me that?'

" 'Lave me alone,' sez Vulmea; 'I'm dyin'!'

" 'I'll wait till you're betther,' sez I, 'an' thin we
two will talk ut out umbrageous.'

"O'Hara pitched Tim into the doolie, none too
tinder, but all the bhoys kep' by their cots, which
was not the sign av innocint men. I was huntin'
ivrywhere for my fallin'-block, but not findin' ut at
all. I niver found ut.

" 'Now fwhat will I do?' sez O'Hara, swinging
the veranda light in his hand an' lookin' down the
room. I had hate an' contimpt av O'Hara an' I
have now, dead tho' he is, but, for all that, will I
say he was a brave man. He is baskin' in purgathory
this tide, but I wish he cud hear that, whin he stud
lookin' down the room an' the bhoys shivered before
the oi av him, I knew him for a brave man an' I
liked him so.

" 'Fwhat will I do?' sez O'Hara ag'in, an' we
heard the voice av a woman low an' sof' in the veranda. 'Twas Slimmy's wife, come over at the shot,

sittin' on wan av the benches an' scarce able to walk.

" 'Oh, Denny—Denny dear,' sez she, 'have they kilt you?'

"O'Hara looked down the room again an' showed his teeth to the gum. Then he spat on the flure.

" 'You're not worth ut,' sez he. 'Light that lamp, ye dogs,' an' wid that he turned away, an' I saw him walkin' off wid Slimmy's wife; she thryin' to wipe off the powther-black on the front av his jackut wid her handkerchief. 'A brave man you are,' thinks I—'a brave man an' a bad woman.'

"No wan said a word for a time. They was all ashamed, past spache.

" 'Fwhat d'you think he will do?' sez wan av thim at last. 'He knows we're all in ut.'

" 'Are we so?' sez I from my cot. 'The man that sez that to me will be hurt. I do not know,' sez I, 'fwhat onderhand divilmint you have con-thrived, but by what I've seen I know that you can not commit murdher wid another man's rifle—such shakin' cowards you are. I'm goin' to slape,' I sez, 'an' you can blow my head off whoile I lay.' I did not slape, though, for a long time. Can ye wonder?

"Next morn the news was through all the rig'-mint, an' there was nothin' that the men did not tell. O'Hara reports, fair an' easy, that Vulmea was come to grief through tamperin' wid his rifle

in barricks, all for to show the mechanism. An'
by my sowl, he had the impart'nince to say that
he was on the shpot at the time an' cud certify that
ut was an accident! You might ha' knocked my
roomful down wid a straw whin they heard that.
'Twas lucky for thim that the bhoys were always
thryin' to find out how the new rifle was made, an'
a lot of thim had come up for easin' the pull by
shtickin' bits av grass an' such in the part av the lock
that showed near the thrigger. The first issues of
the 'Tinis was not covered in, an' I mesilf have eased
the pull av mine time an' ag'in. A light pull is ten
points on the range to me.

"'I will not have this foolishness!' sez the colonel.
'I will twist the tail off Vulmea!' sez he; but whin
he saw him, all tied up an' groanin' in hospital, he
changed his mind. 'Make him an early convales-
cint,' sez he to the doctor, an' Vulmea was made so
for a warnin'. His big bloody bandages an' face
puckered up to wan side did she more to kape the
bhoys from messin' wid the insides av their rifles
than any punishment.

"O'Hara gave no reason for fwhat he'd said,
an' all my roomful were too glad to inquire tho'
he put his spite upon thim more wearin' than before. Wan day, howiver, he tuk me apart very
polite, for he cud be that at the choosin'.

"'You're a good sodger, tho' you're a damned
insolint man,' sez he.

" 'Fair words, sargints,' sez I, 'or I may be insolent ag'in.'

" ' 'Tis not like you,' sez he, 'to lave your rifle
in the rack widout the breech-pin, for widout the
breech-pin she was whin Vulmea fired. I should
ha' found the break av ut in the eyes av the holes,
else,' he sez.

" 'Sargint,' sez I, 'fwhat wud your life ha' been
worth av the breech-pin had been in place, for, on my
sowl, my life wud be worth just as much to me av I
towld you whether ut was or was not. Be thankful
the bullet was not there,' I sez.

" 'That thrue,' sez he, pulling his mustache; 'but
I do not believe that you, for all your lip, was in
that business.'

" 'Sargint,' sez I, 'I cud hammer the life out av
a man in ten minutes wid my fistes if that man
dishpleased me; for I am a good sodger, an' I will
be threated as such, an' whoile my fistes are my
own they're strong enough for all work I have to
do. They do not fly back towards me!' sez I, lookin'
him betune the eyes.

" 'You're a good man,' sez he, lookin' me betune
the eyes—an' oh, he was a gran' built man to see—
'you're a good man,' he sez, 'an' I cud wish, for the
pure frolic av ut, that I was not a sargint, or that
you were not a privit; an' you will think me no
coward whin I say this thing.'

" 'I do not,' sez I. 'I saw you whin Vulmea

mishandled the rifle. But, sargint,' I sez, 'take the wurrd from me now, spakin' as man to man wid the shtripes off, tho' 'tis little right I have to talk, me being fwhat I am by natur'. This time ye tuk no harm, an' next time ye may not, but, in the ind, so sure as Slimmy's wife came into the veranda, so sure will ye take harm—an' bad harm. Have thought, sargint,' sez I. 'Is ut worth ut?'

"'Ye're a bowld man,' sez he, breathin' hard. 'A very bowld man. But I am a bowld man tu. Do you go your way, Privit Mulvaney, an' I will go mine.'

"We had no further spache thin or afther, but, wan by another, he drafted the twelve av my room out into other rooms an' got thim spread among the comp'nies, for they were not a good breed to live together, an' the comp'ny orf'cers saw ut. They wud ha' shot me in the night av they had known fwhat I knew; but that they did not.

"An', in the ind, as I said, O'Hara met his death from Rafferty for foolin' wid his wife. He wint his own way too well—Eyah, too well! Shtraight to that affair, widout turnin' to the right or to the lef', he wint, an' may the Lord have mercy on his sowl. Amin!"

"''Ear! 'Ear!" said Ortheris, pointing the moral with a wave of his pipe. "An' this is 'im 'oo would be a bloomin' Vulmea all for the sake of Mullins an' a bloomin' button! Mullins never went after a woman in his life. Mrs. Mullins, she saw 'im one day—"

"Ortheris," I said, hastily, for the romances of Private Ortheris are slightly too daring for publication, "look at the sun. It's a quarter past six!"

"Oh, Lord! Three quarters of an hour for five an' a 'arf miles! We'll 'ave to run like Jimmy O."

The Three Musketeers clambered on to the bridge, and departed hastily in the direction of the cantonment road. When I overtook them I offered them two stirrups and a tail, which they accepted enthusiastically. Ortheris held the tail, and in this manner we trotted steadily through the shadows by an unfrequented road.

At the turn into the cantonment we heard carriage wheels. It was the colonel's barouche, and in it sat the colonel's wife and daughter. I caught a suppressed chuckle, and my beast sprung forward with a lighter step.

The Three Musketeers had vanished into the night.

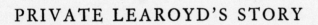

PRIVATE LEAROYD'S STORY

PRIVATE LEAROYD'S STORY

And he told a tale.—*Chronicles of Gautama Buddha.*

FAR from the haunts of Company Officers who insist upon kit-inspections, far from keen-nosed Sergeants who sniff the pipe stuffed into the bedding-roll, two miles from the tumult of the barracks, lies the Trap. It is an old dry well, shadowed by a twisted *pipal* tree and fenced with high grass. Here, in the years gone by, did Private Ortheris establish his depot and menagerie for such possessions, living and dead, as could not safely be introduced to the barrack-room. Here were gathered Houdin pullets, and fox-terriers of undoubted pedigree and more than doubtful ownership, for Ortheris was an inveterate poacher and pre-eminent among a regiment of neat-handed dog-stealers.

Never again will the long lazy evenings return wherein Ortheris, whistling softly moved surgeon-wise among the captives of his craft at the bottom of the well; when Learoyd sat in the niche, giving sage counsel on the management of "tykes," and Mulvaney, from the crook of the overhanging pipal, waved his enormous boots in benediction above our heads, delighted us with tales of love and war, and strange experiences of cities and men.

Ortheris—landed at last in the "little stuff bird-shop" for which your soul longed; Learoyd—back again in the smoky, stone-ribbed north, amid the clang of the Bradford looms; Mulvaney—grizzled, tender, and very wise Ulysses, sweltering on the earth-work of a Central India line—judge if I have forgotten old days in the Trap!

Orth'ris as allus think he knaws more than other foaks, said she wasn't a real laady, but nob-but a Hewrasian. I don't gainsay as her culler was a bit doosky like. But she was a laady. Why, she rode iv a carriage, an' good 'osses, too, an' her 'air was that oiled as you could see your faice in it, an' she wore di'mond rings an' a goold chain, an' silk an' satin dresses as mun 'a' cost a deal, for it isn't a cheap shop as keeps enough o' one pattern to fit a figure like hers. Her name was Mrs. De Sussa, an' t' waay I coom to be acquainted wi' her was along of our colonel's laady's dog Rip.

I've seen a vast o' dogs, but Rip was t' prettiest picter of a cliver fox-tarrier 'at iver I set eyes on. He could do owt you like but speaak, an' t' colonel's laady set more store by him than if he had been a Christian. She hed bairns of her awn, but they was i' England, and Rip seemed to get all t' coddlin' and pettin' as belonged to a bairn by good right.

But Rip were a bit on a rover, an' hed a habit o' breakin' out o' barricks like, and trottin' round t' plaice as if he were t' cantonment magistrate coom round inspectin'. The colonel leathers him once or twice, but Rip didn't care, an' kept on gooin' his rounds, wi' his taail a-waggin' as if he were flag-signalin' to t' world at large 'at he was "gettin' on nicely, thank you, and how's yo'sen?" An' then t' colonel, as was noa sort of a hand wi' a dog, tees him oop. A real clipper of a dog, an' it's noa wonder yon laady, Mrs. De Sussa, should tek a fancy tiv him. Theer's one o' t' Ten Commandments says yo' maun't cuvvet your neebor's ox nor his jackass, but it doesn't say nowt about his tarrier-dogs, an' happen thot's t' reason why Mrs. De Sussa cuvveted Rip, thou' she went to church reg'lar along wi' her husband, who was so mich darkker 'at if he hedn't such a good coaat tiv his back you' might ha' called him a black man, and nut tell a lee naw-ther. They said he addled his brass i' jute, an' he'd a rare lot on it.

Well, you seen, when they teed Rip up, t' poor awd lad didn't enjoy very good 'elth. So t' colonel's laady sends for me as 'ad a naame for bein' knowledgeable about a dog, an' axes what's ailin' wi' him.

"Why," said I, "he's getten t' mopes, an' what he wants is libbaty an' coompany like t' rest on us; wal happens a rat or two 'ud liven him oop. It's low, mum," says I, "is rats, but it's t' nature

of a dog; an' soa's cuttin' round an' meeting another dog or two an' passin' t' time o' day, an'
hevvin' a bit of a turn-up wi' him like a Christian."

So she says her dog maunt niver fight an' noa
Christians iver fought.

"Then what's a soldier for?" says I; an' I ex-
plains to her t' contrairy qualities of- a dog, 'at,
when yo' coom to think on't, is one o' t' curusest
things as is. For they larn to behave theirsens
like gentlemen born, fit for t' fost o' coompany—
they tell me t' widdy herself is fond of a good dog
and knaws one when she sees it as well as onnybody: then on t' other hand a-tewin' round after
cats an' gettin' mixed oop i' all manners o' black-
guardly street rows, an' killin' rats, an' fightin' like
divils.

T' colonel's laady says: "Well, Learoyd, I doan't
agre wi' you, but you're right in a way o' speakin',
an' I should like yo' to tek Rip out a-walkin' wi'
you sometimes; but yo' maunt let him fight, nor
chase cats, nor do nowt 'orrid:" an' them was her
very wo'ds.

Soa Rip an' me gooes out a-walkin' o' evenin's,
he bein' a dog as did credit tiv a man, an' I catches
a lot o' rats an' we hed a bit of a match on in an
awd dry swimmin'-bath at back o' t' cantonments,
an' it was none so long afore he was as bright as a
button again. He hed a way o' flyin' at them big
yaller pariah dogs as if he was a harrow offan a

bow, an' though his weight were nowt, he tuk 'em so suddint-like they rolled over like skittles in a halley, an' when they coot he stretched after 'em as if he were rabbit-runnin'. Saame with cats when he cut get t' cat agaate o' runnin'.

One evenin', him an' me was trespassin' ovver a compound wall after one of them mongooses 'at he'd started, an' we was busy grubbin' round a prickle-bush, an' when we looks up there was Mrs. De Sussa wi' a parasel ovver her shoulder, a-watchin' us. "Oh, my!" she sings out; "there's that love-lee dog! Would he let me stroke him, Mister Soldier?"

"Ay he would, mum," sez I, "for he's fond o' laady's coompany. Coom here, Rip, an' speak to this kind laady." An' Rip, seein' 'at t' mongoose hed gotten clean awaay, cooms up like t' gentle-man he was, nivver a hauporth shy nor okkord.

"Oh, you beautiful—you prettee dog!" she says, clippin' an' chantin' her speech in a way them sooart has o' their awn; "I would like a dog like you. You are so verree lovelee—so awfullee prettee," an' all thot sort o' talk, 'at a dog o' sense mebbe thinks nowt on, tho' he bides it by reason o' his breedin'.

An' then I meks him joomp ovver my swagger-cane, an' shek hands, an' beg, an' lie dead, an' a lot o' them tricks as laadies teeaches dogs, though I doan't haud with it mysen, for it's makin' a fool o' a good dog to do such like.

An' at lung length it cooms out 'at she'd been thrawin' sheep's eyes, as t' sayin' is, at Rip for many a day. Yo' see, her childer was grown up, an' she'd nowt mich to do, an' were allus fond of a dog. Soa she axes me if I'd tek somethin' to dhrink. An' we goes into t' drawn-room wheer her 'usband was a-settin'. They meks a gurt fuss ovver t' dog, an' I had a bottle o' aale, an' he gave me a handful o' cigars.

Soa I coomed away, but t' awd lass sings out: "Oh, Mister Soldier! please coom again and bring that prettee dog."

I didn't let on to t' colonel's lady about Mrs. De Sussa, and Rip, he says nowt nawther; an' I gooes again, an' ivry time there was a good dhrink an' a handful o' good smooaks. An' I telled t' awd lass a heep more about Rip than I'd ever heeared; how he tuk t' fost prize at Lunnon dogshow and cost thotty-three pounds fower shillin' from t' man as bred him; 'at his own brother was t' propputty o' t' Prince o' Wailes, an' 'at he had a pedigree as long as a dook's. An' she lapped it all oop an' were nivir tired o' admirin' him. But when t' awd lass took to givin' me money an' I seed 'at she were gettin' fair fond about t' dog, I began to suspicion summat. Onnybody may give a soldier t' price of a pint in a friendly way an' theer's no 'arm done, but when it cooms to five rupees slipt into your hand, sly like, why, it's what t' 'lectioneerin' fellows calls bribery an' corruption. Specially when Mrs. De Sussa threwed hints how t' cold weather would soon be ovver an' she was goin' to Munsooree Pahar, an' we was goin' to Rawalpindi, an' she would nivir see Rip any more onless somebody she knowed on would be kind tiv her.

Soa I tells Mulvaney an' Ortheris all t' taale thro', beginnin' to end.

"'Tis larceny that wicked ould laady manes," says t' Irishman, "'tis felony she is sejjuicin' ye into, my friend Learoyd, but I'll purtect your innocince. I'll save ye from the wicked wiles av that wealthy ould woman, an' I'll go wid ye this evenin' and spake to her the wurrds ave truth an' honesty. But Jock," says he, waggin' his heead, "'twas not like ye to kape all that good dhrink an' thim fine cigars to yerself, while Orth'ris here an' me have been prowin' round with throats as dry as lime-kilns, and nothin' to smoke but canteen plug. 'Twas a dhirty thrick to play on a comrade, for why should you, Learoyd, be balancin' yourself on the butt av a satin chair, as if Terence Mulvaney was not the aquil av anybody who thrades in jute!"

"Let alone me," sticks in Orth'ris; "but that's like life. Them wot's really fitted to decorate society get no show, while a blunderin' Yorkshireman like you—"

"Nay," says I, "it's none o' t' blunderin' York-shireman she wants, it's Rip. He's t' gentleman this journey."

Soa t' next day, Mulvaney an' Rip an' me goes to Mrs. De Sussa's, an' t' Irishman bein' a strainger she wor a bit shy at fost. But you've heard Mulvaney talk, an' yo' may believe as he fairly be-witched t' awd lass wal she let out 'at she wanted to tek Rip away wi' her to Munsooree Pahar. Then Mulvaney changes his tune an' axes her solemn-like if she'd thonught o' t' consequences o' gettin' two poor but honest soldiers sent t' Andamning Islands. Mrs. De Sussa began to cry, so Mulvaney turns round oppen t' other tack and smooths her down, allowin' 'at Rip ud be a vast better off in t' hills than down i' Bengal, and 'twas a pity he shouldn't go wheer he was so well beliked. And soa he went on, backin' and' fillin' an workin' up t' awd lass wal she felt as if her life warn't worth nowt if she didn't hev t' dog.

Then all of a suddint he says: "But ye shall have him, marm, for I've a feelin' heart, not like this cowld-blooded Yorkshireman; but 'twill cost ye not a penny less than three hundher rupees."

"Don't you believe him, mum," says I; "t' colo-nel's laady wouldn't tek five hundred for him."

"Who said she would?" says Mulvaney; "it's not buyin' him I mane, but for the sake o' this kind, good laady, I'll do what I never dreamt to do in my life. I'll stale him!"

"Don't say steal," says Mrs. De Sussa; "he shall have the happiest home. Dogs often get lost, you know, and then they stray, an' he likes me, and I like him as I niver liked a dog yet, an' I must hev him. If I got him at t' last minute I could carry him off to Munsooree Pahar and nobody would niver knaw."

Now an' again Mulvaney looked acrost at me, an' though I could make nowt o' what he was after, I concluded to take his leead.

"Well, mum," I says, "I never thowt to coom down to dog-stealin', but if my comrade sees how it could be done to oblige a laady like yo'sen, I'm nut t' man to hod back, tho' it's a bad business, I'm thinkin', an' three hundred rupees is a poor set-off again t' chance of them Damning Islands as Mulvaney talks on."

"I'll mek it three fifty," says Mrs. De Sussa; "only let me hev t' dog!"

So we let her persuade us, an' she teks Rip's measure theer an' then, an' sent to Hamilton's to order a silver collar again t' time when he was to be her awn, which was to be t' day she set off for Munsooree Pahar.

"Sitha, Mulvaney," says I, when we was outside, "you're niver goin' to let her hev Rip!"

"An' would ye disappoint a poor ould woman?" says he; "she shall have *a* Rip."

"An' wheer's he to come through?" says I.

"Learoyd, my man," he sings out, "you're a

pretty man av your inches an' a good comrade, but your head is made av duff. Isn't our friend Orth'ris a taxidermist, an' a rale artist wid his nimble white fingers? An' what's a taxidermist but a man who can thrate skins? Do ye mind the white dog that belongs to the canteen sargint, bad cess to him —he that's lost half his time an' snarling the rest? He shall be lost for good now; an' do ye mind that he's the very spit in shape an' size av the colonel's, barrin' that his tail is an inch too long, an' he has none av the color that divarsifies the rale Rip, an' his timper is that av his masther an' worse. But fwhat is an inch on a dog's tail? An' fwhat to a professional like Orth'ris is a few ring-straked shpots av black, brown, an' white? Nothin' at all, at all."

Then we meets Orth'ris, an' that little man, bein' as sharp as a needle, seed his way through t' business in a minute. An' he went to work a-practicin' 'air-dyes the very next day, beginnin' on some white rabbits he had, an' then he drored all Rip's markin's on t' back of a white commissariat bullock, so as to get his 'and in an' be sure of his colors; shadin' off brown into black as nateral as life. If Rip had a fault it was too mich markin', but it was straingely reg'lar, an' Orth'ris settled himself to make a fost-rate job on it when he got haud o' t' canteen sargint's dog. Theer niver was sich a dog as thot for bad temper, an' it did nut get no better when his tail hed to be fettled an inch an' a half shorter. But they may talk o' theer Royal Academies as they like, I niver seed a bit o' animal paintin' to beat t' copy as Orth'ris made of Rip's marks, wal' t' picter itself was snarlin' all t' time an' tryin' to get at Rip standin' theer to be copied as good as goold.

Orth'ris allus hed as mich conceit on himsen as would lift a balloon, an' he wor so pleeased wi' his sham Rip he wor for tekking him to Mrs. De Sussa before she went away. But Mulvaney an' me stopped thot, knowin' Orth'ris work, though niver so cliver, was nobbut skin-deep. An' at last Mrs. De Sussa fixed t' day for startin' to Munsooree Pahar. We was to tek Rip to t' stayshun i' a basket an' hand him ovver just when they was ready to start, an' then she'd give us t' brass—as was agreed upon.

An' my wo'd! It were high time she were off, for them 'air-dyes upon t' curs back took a vast of paintin' to keep t' reet culler, tho' Arth'ris spent a matter of seven rupees six annas i' t' best drooggist shops i' Calcutta.

An' t' canteen sergeant was lookin' for 'is dog everywheer; an', wi' bein' tied up, t' beast's timper got waur nor ever.

It wor i' t' evenin' when t' train started thro' Howrah, an' we 'elped Mrs. De Sussa wi' about sixty boxes, an' then we gave her t' basket. Or-

th'ris, for pride av his work, axed us to let him coom
along wi' us, an' he couldn't help liftin' t' lid an'
showin' t' cur as he lay coiled oop.

"Oh!" says t' awd lass; "the beautee! How
sweet he looks!" An' just then t' beauty snarled
an' showed his teeth, so Mulvaney shuts down t'
lid and says: "Ye'll be careful, marm, whin ye
tek him out. He's disaccustomed to traveling by t'
railway, an' he'll be sure to want his rale mistress an' his friend Learoyd, so ye'll make allowance for his feelings at fost."

She would do all thot an' more for the dear,
good Rip, an' she would nut oppen t' basket till
they were miles away, for fear anybody should recognize him, an' we were real good and kind soldier-
men, we were, an' she honds me a bundle o' notes,
an' then cooms up a few of her relations an' friends
to say good-by—not more than seventy-five there
wasn't—an' we cuts away.

What coom to t' three hundred and fifty rupees?
Thot's what I can scarcelins tell you, but we melted
it. It was share an' share alike, for Mulvaney said:
"If Learoyd got hold of Mrs. De Sussa first, sure
'twas I that remimbered the sargint's dog just in
the nick av time, an' Orth'ris was the artist av janius
that made a work av art out av that ugly piece av
ill-nature. Yet, by way av a thank-offerin' that I
was not led into felony by that wicked ould woman,
I'll send a thrifle a Father Victor for the poor
people he's always beggin' for."

But me an' Orth'ris, he bein' cockney an' I bein' pretty far north, did nut see it i' t' saame way. We'd getten t' brass, an' we meaned to keep it. An' soa we did—for a short time.

Noa, noa, we niver heard a wod more o' t' awd lass. Our rig'mint went to Pindi, an' t' canteen sargint he got himself another tyke insteead o' t' one 'at got lost so reg'lar, an' was lost for good at last.

THE BIG DRUNK DRAF'

THE BIG DRUNK DRAF'

> We're goin' 'ome, we're goin' 'ome—
> Our ship is *at* the shore,
> An' you mus' pack your 'aversack,
> For we won't come back no more.
> Ho, don't you grieve for me,
> My lovely Mary Ann,
> For I'll marry you yet on a fourp'ny bit,
> As a time-expired ma-a-an!
> —*Barrack Room Ballad.*

An awful thing has happened! My friend, Private Mulvaney, who went home in the "Serapis," time-expired, not very long ago, has come back to India as a civilian! It was all Dinah Shadd's fault. She could not stand the poky little lodgings, and she missed her servant Abdullah more than words could tell. The fact was that the Mulvaneys had been out here too long, and had lost touch of England.

Mulvaney knew a contractor on one of the new Central India lines, and wrote to him for some sort of work. The contractor said that if Mulvaney could pay the passage he would give him command of a gang of coolies for old sake's sake. The pay was eighty-five rupees a month, and Dinah Shadd said that if Terence did not accept she would

make his life a "basted purgathory." There-
fore the Mulvaneys came out as "civilians," which
was a great and terrible fall; though Mulvaney tried
to disguise it, by saying that he was "ker'nel on the
railway line, an' a consequinshal man."

He wrote me an invitation, on a tool-indent form,
to visit him; and I came down to the funny little
"construction" bungalow at the side of the line.
Dinah Shadd had planted peas about and about,
and nature had spread all manner of green stuff
round the place. There was no change in Mulvaney except the change of raiment, which was de-
plorable, but could not be helped. He was standing
upon his trolley, haranguing a gang-man, and his
shoulders were as well drilled, and his big, thick
chin was as clean-shaven as ever.

"I'm a civilian now," said Mulvaney. "Cud
you tell that I was iver a martial man? Don't
answer, sorr, av you're a strainin' betune a com-
pliment an' a lie. There's no houldin' Dinah
Shadd now she's got a house av her own. Go inside, an' dhrink tay out av chiny in the drrrraw-
in'-room, an' thin we'll dhrink like Christians
undher the tree here. Scut, ye naygur-folk!
There's a sahib come to call on me, an' that's more
than he'll iver do for you onless you run! Get
out, an' go on pilin' up the earth, quick, till sundown."

When we three were comfortably settled under

the big *sisham* in front of the bungalow, and the first rush of questions and answers about Privates Ortheris and Learoyd and old times and places had died away, Mulvaney said, reflectively: "Glory be there's no p'rade to-morrow, an' no bun-headed corp'ril-bhoy to give you his lip. An' yit I don't know. 'Tis harrd to be something ye niver were an' niver meant to be, an' all the ould days shut up along wid your papers. Eyah! I'm growin' rusty, an' 'tis the will av God that a man mustn't serve his quane for time an' all."

He helped himself to a fresh peg, and sighed furiously.

"Let your beard grow, Mulvaney," said I, "and then you won't be troubled with those notions. You'll be a real civilian."

Dinah Shadd had confided to me in the drawing-room her desire to coax Mulvaney into letting his beard grow. " 'Twas so civilian-like," said poor Dinah, who hated her husband's hankering for his old life.

"Dinah Shadd, you're a dishgrace to an honest, clane-scraped man!" said Mulvaney, without replying to me. "Grow a beard on your own chin, darlint, and lave my razors alone. They're all that stand betune me and dis-ris-pect-ability. Av I didn't shave, I wud be torminted wid an outrajis thurrst; for there's nothin' so dhryin' to the throat as a big billy-goat beard waggin' undher the chin. Ye wudn't have me dhrink always, Dinah Shadd? By the same token, you're kapin me crool dhry now. Let me look at that whisky."

The whisky was lent and returned, but Dinah Shadd, who had been just as eager as her husband in asking after old friends, rent me with:

"I take shame for you, sorr, comin' down here —though the saints know you're as welkim as the daylight whin you do come—an' upsettin' Terence's head wid your nonsense about—about fwhat's much better forgotten. He bein' a civilian now, an' you niver was aught else. Can you not let the arrmy rest? 'Tis not good for Terence."

I took refuge by Mulvaney, for Dinah Shadd has a temper of her own.

"Let be—let be," said Mulvaney. " 'Tis only wanst in a way I can talk about the ould days." Then to me: "Ye say Dhrumshticks is well, an' his lady tu? I niver knew how I liked the gray garron till I was shut av him an' Asia." ("Dhrumshticks" was the nickname of the colonel commanding Mulvaney's old regiment.) "Will you be seein' him again? You will. Thin tell him"—Mulvaney's eyes began to twinkle—"tell him wid Privit—"

"Mister, Terence," interrupted Dinah Shadd.

"Now the divil an' all his angels an' the firmament av hiven fly away wid the 'Mister,' an' the sin av makin' me swear be on your confession, Dinah Shadd! Privit, I tell ye. Wid Privit Mulvaney's best obedience, that but for me the last time-expired wud be still pullin' hair on their way to the sea."

He threw himself back in the chair, chuckled, and was silent.

"Mrs. Mulvaney," I said, "please take up the whisky, and don't let him have it until he has told the story."

Dinah Shadd dexterously whipped the bottle away, saying at the same time, "'Tis nothing to be proud av," and thus captured by the enemy, Mulvaney spake:

"'Twas on Chuseday week. I was behaderin' round wid the gangs on the 'bankmint—I've taught the hoppers how to kape step an' stop screechin'— whin a head-gangman comes up to me, wid about two inches av shirt-tail hanging round his neck an' a disthressful light in his oi. 'Sahib,' sez he, 'there's a reg'mint an' a half av soldiers up at the junction, knockin' red cinders out av ivrything an' ivrybody! They thried to hang me in my cloth,' he sez, 'an' there will be murder an' ruin an' rape in the place before nightfall! They say they're coming down here to wake us up. What will we do wid our women-folk?"

"'Fetch my throlly!' sez I; 'my heart's sick in my ribs for a wink at anything wid the quane's uniform on ut. Fetch my throlly, an' six av the jildiest men, and run me up in shtyle.'"

"He tuk his best coat," said Dinah Shadd re-proachfully.

"'Twas to do honor to the widdy. I cud ha' done no less, Dinah Shadd. You and your di-greshins interfere wid the coorse av the narrative. Have you iver considhered fwhat I wud look like wid me head shaved as well as my chin? You bear that in your mind, Dinah darlin'.

"I was throllied up six miles, all to get a shquint at that draf'. I knew 'twas a spring draf' goin' home, for there's no rig'mint hereabout, more's the pity."

"Praise the Virgin!" murmured Dinah Shadd. But Mulvaney did not hear.

"Whin I was about three quarters av a mile off the rest-camp, powtherin' along fit to burrst, I heard the noise av the men, an', on my sowl, sorr, I cud catch the voice av Peg Barney bellowin' like a bison wid the bellyache. You remember Peg Barney that was in D comp'ny—a red, hairy scraun, wid a scar on his jaw? Peg Barney that cleared out the Blue Lights' Jubilee meeting wid the cook-room mop last year?

"Thin I knew ut was a draf' of the ould rig'-mint, an' I was conshumed wid sorrow for the bhoy that was in charge. We was harrd scrapin's at any time. Did I iver tell you how Horker Kelley went into clink nakid as Phœbus Apollonius, wid the shirts av the corp'ril an' file undher his arrum? An' he was a moild man! But I'm digreshin'. 'Tis a

shame both to the rig'mints and the arrmy sendin'
down little orf'cer bhoys wid a draf' av strong men
mad wid liquor an' the chanst av gettin shut av India,
an' niver a punishment that's fit to be given right
down an' away from cantonmints to the dock! 'Tis
this nonsince. Whin I am servin' my time, I'm
undher the articles av war, an' can be whipped on the
peg for thim. But whin I've served my time, I'm
a Reserve man an' the articles av war haven't any
hould on me. An orf'cer can't do anythin' to a time-
expired savin' confinin' him to barricks. 'Tis a wise
rig'lation, bekaze a time-expired does not have any
barricks; bein' on the move all the time. 'Tis a
Solomon av a rig'lation, is that. I wud like to be
inthroduced to the man who secreted ut. 'Tis easier
to get colts from a Kibbereen horse-fair into Galway
than to take a bad draf over ten miles av country.
Consiquintly that rig'lation for fear that the men
wud be hurt by the little orf'cer bhoy. No matther.
The nearer my throlly came to the rest-camp, the
woilder was the shine, an' the louder was the voice
av Peg Barney. ' 'Tis good I am here,' thinks I to
myself, 'for Peg alone is employmint to two or three.'
He bein', I well knew, as copped as a dhrover.

"Faith, that rest-camp was a sight! The tent-
ropes was all skew-nosed, an' the pegs looked as
dhrunk as the men—fifty av thim—the scourin's,
an' rinsin's, an' divil's lavin's av the ould rig'-
mint. I tell you, sorr, they were dhrunker than any
men you've ever seen in your mortial life. How

does a draf' get dhrunk? How does a frog get fat? They suk ut in through their shkins.

"There was Peg Barney sittin' on the groun' in his shirt—wan shoe off an' wan shoe on—whackin' a tent-peg over the head wid his boot, an' singin' fit to wake the dead. 'Twas no clane song that he sung, tho'. 'Twas the 'Divil's Mass.' "

"What's that?" I asked.

"Whin a bad egg is shut av the arrmy, he sings the 'Divils Mass' for a good riddance; an' that manes swearin' at ivrything from the command-her-in-chief down to the room-corp'ril, such as you niver in your days heard. Some men can swear so as to make green turf crack! Have you iver heard the curse in an Orange lodge? The 'Divil's Mass' is ten times worse, an' Peg Barney was singin' ut, whackin' the tent-peg on the head wid his boot for each man that he cursed. A powerful big voice had Peg Barney, an' a hard swearer he was whin sober. I stood forninst him, an' 'twas not me oi alone that cud tell Peg was dhrunk as a coot.

" 'Good-morning', Peg,' I sez, whin he dhrew breath afther cursin' the adj'tint-gen'ral; 'I've put on my best coat to see you, Peg Barney,' sez I.

" 'Thin take ut off again,' sez Peg Barney, lather-in' away wid the boot; 'take ut off an' dance, ye lousy civilian!'

"Wid that he begins cursing' ould Dhrumshticks, being so full he clean misremembers the brigade-major an' the advokit gen'ral.

"'Do you not know me, Peg?' sez I, though me blood was hot in me wid bein' called a civilian."

"An' him a decent married man!" wailed Dinah.

"'I do not,' sez Peg, 'but dhrunk or sober I'll tear the hide off your back wid a shovel whin I've stopped singin'.'

"'Say you so, Peg Barney?' sez I. ''Tis clear as mud you've forgotten me. I'll assist your auto-biography.' Wid that I stretched Peg Barney, boot an' all, an' wint into the camp. An awful sight ut was!

"'Where's the orf'cer in charge av the detach-ment?' sez I to Scrub Greene—the manest little worm that ever walked.

"'There's no orf'cer, ye ould cook,' sez Scrub; 'we're a bloomin' republic.'

"'Are you that?' sez I; 'thin I'm O'Connell the Dictator, an' by this you will larn to kape a civil tongue in your rag-box.'

"Wid that I stretched Scrub Green an' wint to the orf'cer's tent. 'Twas a new little bhoy—not wan I'd iver seen before. He was sittin' in his tent, pur-tendin' not to 'ave ear av the racket.

"I saluted—but for the life av me I mint to shake hands whin I went in. 'Twas the sword hangin' on the tent-pole changed my will.

"'Can't I help, sorr?' sez I; ''tis a strong man's job they've given you, an' you'll be wantin' help by sundown.' He was a bhoy wid bowils, that child, an' a rale gintleman.

" 'Sit down,' sez he.

" 'Not before my orf'cer,' sez I; an' I tould him fwhat my service was.

" 'I've heard av you,' sez he. 'You tuk the town av Lungtungpen nakid.'

" 'Faith,' thinks I, 'that's honor an' glory'; for 'twas Lift'nint Brazenose did that job. 'I'm wid ye, sorr,' sez I, 'if I'm av use. They shud niver ha' sent you down wid the draf'. Savin' your presince, sorr,' I sez, ' 'tis only Lift'nint Hackerston in the ould reg'mint can manage a home draf'.'

" 'I've niver had charge of men like this before,' sez he, playin' wid the pens on the table; 'an' I see by the rig'lations——'

" 'Shut your oi to the rig'lations, sorr,' I sez, 'till the throoper's into blue wather. By the rig'lations you've got to tuck thim up for the night, or they'll be runnin' foul av my coolies an' makin' a shiver-arium half through the country. Can you trust your non-coms, sorr?'

" 'Yes,' sez he.

" 'Good,' sez I; 'there'll be throuble before the night. Are you marchin', sorr?'

" 'To the next station,' sez he.

" 'Better still,' sez I; 'there'll be big throuble.'

" 'Can't be too hard on a home draf',' sez he; 'the great thing is to get thim in-ship.'

" 'Faith, you've learnt the half av your lesson, sorr,' sez I, 'but av you shtick to the rig'lations you'll niver get thim in-ship at all, at all. Or there won't be a rag av kit betune thim whin you do.'

" 'Twas a dear little orf'cer bhoy, an' by way av kapin' his heart up, I tould him fwhat I saw wanst in a draf' in Egypt."

"What was that, Mulvaney?" said I.

"Sivin-an'-fifty men sittin' on the bank av a canal, laughin' at a poor little squidgereen av an orf'cer that they'd made wade into the slush an' pitch the things out av the boats for their lord high mightinesses. That made the orf'cer bhoy woild wid indignation.

" 'Soft an' aisy, sorr,' sez I; 'you've niver had your draf' in hand since you left cantonmints. Wait till the night, an' your work will be ready to you. Wid you permission, sorr, I will investigate the camp, an' talk to my ould frins. 'Tis no manner av use thryin' to shtop the divilmint now.'

"Wid that I wint out into the camp an' inthrojuced mysilf to ivry man sober enough to remimber me. I was some wan in the ould days, an' the bhoys was glad to see me—all excipt Peg Barney, wid a eye like a tomato five days in the bazaar, an' a nose to correspon'. They come round me an' shuk me, an' I tould thim I was in privit employ wid an income av me own, an' a drrrawin'-room fit to bate the quane's; an' wid me lies an' me shtories an' nonsince ginrally I kept 'em quiet in wan way an' another, knockin' roun' the camp. 'Twas bad even thin whin I was the Angil av Peace.

"I talked to me ould non-coms—they was sober —an' betune me an' thim we wore the draf' over into their tents at the proper time. The little orf'cer bhoy he comes round, decint an' civil-spoken as might be.

" 'Rough quarters, men,' sez he, 'but you can't look to be as comfortable as in barricks. We must make the best av things. I've shut my eyes to a dale av dog's tricks to-day, an' now there must be no more av ut.'

" 'No more we will. Come an' have a dhrink, me son,' sez Peg Barney, staggerin' where he stud. Me little orf'cer bhoy kep his timper.

" 'You're a sulky swine, you are,' sez Peg Barney, an' at that the men in the tent began to laugh.

"I tould you me orf'cer bhoy had bowils. He cut Peg Barney as near as might be on the oi that I'd squashed whin we first met. Peg wint spinnin' acrost the tent.

" 'Peg him out, sorr,' sez I, in a whisper.

" 'Peg him out!' sez me orf'cer bhoy, up loud, just as if 'twas battalion p'rade, an' he pickin' his wurrds from the sargint.

"The non-coms tuk Peg Barney—a howlin' handful he was—an' in three—minutes he was pegged out—chin down, tight-dhrawn—on his stummick, a peg to each arm an' leg, swearin' fit to turn a naygur white.

"I tuk a peg an' jammed ut into his ugly jaw. 'Bite on that Peg Barney,' I sez; 'the night is settin' frosty, an' you'll be wantin' divarsion before the mornin'. But for the rig'lations you'd be bitin' on a bullet now at the thriangles, Peg Barney,' sez I.

"All the draf' was out av their tents watchin' Barney bein' pegged.

"''Tis ag'in the rig'lations! He strook him!' screeches out Scrub Greene, who was always a lawyer; an' some of the men tuk up the shoutin'.

"'Peg out that man!' sez me orf'cer bhoy, niver losin' his timper; an' the non-coms wint in and pegged out Scrub Greene by the side av Peg Barney.

"I could see that the draf' was comin' roun'. The men stud not knowing fwhat to do.

"'Get to your tents!' sez me orf'cer bhoy. 'Sargint, put a sintry over these two men.'

"The men wint back into the tents like jackals, an' the rest av the night there was no noise at all excipt the stip av the sintry over the two, an' Scrub Greene blubberin' like a child. 'Twas a chilly night, an' faith ut sobered Peg Barney.

"Just before revelly, me orf'cer bhoy comes out an' sez: 'Loose those men an' send thim to their tents!' Scrub Greene wint away widout a word, but Peg Barney, stiff wid the cowld, stud like a sheep, thryin' to make his orf'cer undershtand he was sorry for playing the goat.

"There was no tucker in the draf' whin ut fell in for the march, an' divil a wurrd about 'illegality' could I hear.

"I wint to the ould color sargint and I sez: 'Let me die in glory,' sez I. 'I've seen a man this day!'

"'A man he is,' sez ould Hother; 'the draf's as sick as a herrin'. They'll all go down to the sea like lambs. That bhoy has the bowils av a cantonmint av gin'rals.'

"'Amin,' sez I, 'an' good luck go wid him, wheriver he be, by land or by say. Let me know how the draf' gets clear.'

"An' do you know how they did? That bhoy, so I was tould by letter from Bombay, bully-damned 'em down to the dock, till they cudn't call their sowls their own. From the time they left me oi till they was 'tween decks, not wan av thim was more than dacintly dhrunk. An', by the holy articles av war, whin they wint aboard they cheered him till they cudn't spake, an' that, mark you, has not come about wid a draf' in the mim'ry av livin' man! You look to that little orf'cer bhoy. He has bowils. 'Tis not ivry child that wud chuck the rig'lations to Flanders an' stretch Peg Barney on a wink from a brokin an' dilapidated ould carkiss like mesilf. I'd be proud to serve——"

"Terence, you're a civilian," said Dinah Shadd warningly.

"So I am——so I am. Is ut likely I wud forget ut? But he was a gran' bhoy all the same, an' I'm only a mudtipper wid a hot on my shoulthers. The whisky's in the heel av your hand, Sorr. Wid your good lave we'll dhrink to the Ould Rig'mint—three fingers—standin' up!"

And we drank.

ONLY A SUBALTERN

ONLY A SUBALTERN

. . . . Not only to enforce by command but to encourage by example the energetic discharge of duty and the steady endurance of the difficulties and privations inseparable from Military Service.—*Bengal Army Regulations.*

THEY made Bobby Wick pass an examination at Sandhurst. He was a gentleman before he was gazetted, so, when the empress announced that "Gentleman-Cadet Robert Hanna Wick" was posted as second lieutenant to the Tyneside Tail Twisters at Krab Bakhar, he became an officer and a gentleman, which is an enviable thing; and there was joy in the house of Wick where Mamma Wick and all the little Wicks fell upon their knees and offered incense to Bobby by virtue of his achievements.

Papa Wick had been a commissioner in his day, holding authority over three millions of men in the Chota-Buldana Division, building great works for the good of the land, and doing his best to make two blades of grass grow where there was but one before. Of course nobody knew anything about this in the little English village where he was just "old Mr. Wick" and had forgotten that he was a Companion of the Order of the Star of India.

He patted Bobby on the shoulder and said: "Well done, my boy!"

There followed, while the uniform was being prepared, an interval of pure delight, during which Bobby took brevet-rank as a "man" at the woman-swamped tennis parties and tea-fights of the village, and, I dare say, had his joining-time been extended, would have fallen in love with several girls at once. Little country villages at home are very full of nice girls, because all the young men come out here to make their fortunes.

"India," said Papa Wick, "is the place. I've had thirty years of it, and, begad, I'd like to go back again. When you join the Tail Twisters you'll be among friends, if every one hasn't forgotten Wick of Chota-Buldana, and a lot of people will be kind to you for our sakes. The men will tell you more about outfit than I can; but remember this. Stick to your regiment, Bobby—stick to your regiment. You'll see men all round you going into the staff corps, and doing every possible sort of duty but regimental, and you may be tempted to follow suit. Now so long as you keep within your allowance—and I haven't stinted you there—stick to the line—the whole line and nothing but the line. Be careful how you back another young fool's bill, and if you fall in love with a woman twenty years older than yourself, don't tell me about it, that's all."

With these counsels, and many others equally valuable, did Papa Wick fortify Bobby ere that last awful night at Portsmouth when the officers' quarters held more inmates than were provided for by the regulations, and the liberty-men of the ships fell foul of the drafts for India, and the battle raged long and loud from the dock-yard gates even to the slums of Longport, while the drabs of Fratton came down and scratched the races of the queen's officers.

Bobby Wick, with an ugly bruise on his freckled nose, a sick and shaky detachment to maneuver inship and the comfort of fifty scornful females to attend to, had no time to feel homesick till the "Malabar" reached midchannel, when he combined his emotions with a little guard-visiting and a great deal of nausea.

The Tail Twisters were a most particular regiment. Those who knew them least said that they were eaten up with "side." But their reserve and their internal arrangements generally were merely protective diplomacy. Some five years before, the colonel commanding had looked into the fourteen fearless eyes of seven plump and juicy subalterns who had all applied to enter the staff corps, and had asked them why the three stars should he, a colonel of the line, command a dashed nursery for double-dashed bottle-suckers who put on condemned tin spurs and rode qualified mokes at the hiatused heads of forsaken black regiments. He was a rude man and a terrible. Wherefore the remnant took measures (with the half-butt as an engine of public opinion) till the rumor went abroad that young men who used the Tail Twisters as a crutch to the staff corps had many and varied trials to endure. However, a regiment had just as much right to its own secrets as a woman.

When Bobby came up from Deolali and took his place among the Tail Twisters, it was gently but firmly borne in upon him that the regiment was his father and his mother and his indissolubly wedded wife, and that there was no crime under the canopy of heaven blacker than that of bringing shame on the regiment, which was the best-shooting, best-drilled, best set-up, bravest, most illustrious, and in all respects most desirable regiment within the compass of the seven seas. He was taught the legends of the mess plate, from the great grinning golden gods that had come out of the Summer Palace in Pekin to the silver-mounted markhor-horn snuff-mull presented by the last C. O. (he who spake to the seven subalterns). And every one of those legends told him of battles fought at long odds, without fear as without support; of hospitality catholic as an Arab's; of friendships deep as the sea and steady as the fighting-line; of honor won by hard roads for honor's sake; and of instant and unquestioning devotion to the regiment—the regiment that claims the lives of all and lives forever.

More than once, too, he came officially into contact with the regimental colors, which looked like the lining of a bricklayer's hat on the end of a chewed stick. Bobby did not kneel and worship them, because British subalterns are not constructed in that manner. Indeed, he condemned them for their weight at the very moment that they were filling with awe and other more noble sentiments.

But best of all was the occasion when he moved with the Tail Twisters in review order at the breaking of a November day. Allowing for dutymen and sick, the regiment was one thousand and eighty strong, and Bobby belonged to them; for was not he a subaltern of the line—the whole line, and nothing but the line—as the tramp of two thousand one hundred and sixty sturdy ammunition boots attested? He would not have changed places with Deighton of the horse battery, whirling by in a pillar of cloud to a chorus of "Strong right! Strong left!" or Hogan-Yale of the White Hussars, leading his squadron for all it was worth, with the price of horseshoes thrown in; or "Tick" Bolieau, trying to live up to his fierce blue and gold turban while the wasps of the Bengal Cavalry stretched to a gallop in the wake of the long, lolloping Walers of the White Hussars.

They fought through the clear cool day, and Bobby felt a little thrill run down his spine when he heard the tinkle-tinkle-tinkle of the empty cartridge-cases hopping from the breech-blocks after the roar of the volleys; for he knew that he should live to hear that sound in action. The review ended in a glorious chase across the plain—batteries thundering after cavalry to the huge disgust of the White Hussars, and the Tyneside Tail Twisters hunting a Sikh regiment, till the lean lathy Singhs panted with exhaustion. Bobby was dusty and dripping long before noon, but his enthusiasm was merely focused—not diminished.

He returned to sit at the feet of Revere, his "skipper"—that is to say, the captain of his company, and to be instructed in the dark art and mystery of managing men, which is a very large part of the profession of arms.

"If you haven't a taste that way," said Revere between his puffs on his cheroot, "you'll never be able to get the hang of it, but remember, Bobby, it isn't the best drill, though drill is nearly everything, that hauls a regiment through hell and out on the other side. It's the man who knows how to handle men—goat-men, swine-men, dog-men, and so on."

"Dormer, for instance," said Bobby. "I think he comes under the head of fool-men. He mopes like a sick owl."

"That's where you make your mistake, my son. Dormer isn't a fool yet, but he's a dashed dirty soldier, and his room corporal makes fun of his socks before kit-inspection. Dormer, being two-thirds pure brute, goes into a corner and growls."

"How do you know?" said Bobby, admiringly.

"Because a company commander has to know these things—because if he does not know, he may have crime—ay, murder—brewing under his very nose and yet not see that it's there. Dormer is being badgered out of his mind—big as he is—and he hasn't intellect enough to resent it. He's taken to quiet boozing. Bobby, when the butt of a room goes on the drink, or takes to moping by himself, measures are necessary to yank him out of himself."

"What measures? Man can't run round coddling his men forever."

"No. The men would precious soon show him that he was not wanted. You've got to—"

Here the color-sergeant entered with some papers; Bobby reflected for awhile as Revere looked through the company forms.

"Does Dormer do anything, sergeant?" Bobby asked with the air of one continuing an interrupted conversation.

"No, sir. Does 'is dooty like a hor-tomato," said the sergeant, who delighted in long words. "A dirty soldier, an' 'e's under full stoppages for new kit. It's covered with scales, sir."

"Scales? What scales?"

"Fish scales, sir. 'E's always pokin' in the mud by the river an' a-cleanin' them muchly fish with 'is thumbs." Revere was still absorbed in the company papers, and the sergeant, who was grimly fond of Bobby, continued: " 'E generally goes down there when 'e's got 'is skinful, beggin' your pardon, sir, an' they do say that the more lush—in-he-briated 'e 'is, the more fish 'e catches. They call him the Looney Fishmonger in the comp'ny, sir."

Revere signed the last paper and the sergeant retreated.

"It's a filthy amusement," sighed Bobby to himself. Then aloud to Revere: "Are you really worried about Dormer?"

"A little. You see he's never mad enough to send to hospital, or drunk enough to run in, but at any minute he may flare up, brooding and sulking as he does. He resents any interest being shown in him, and the only time I took him out shooting he all but shot me by accident."

"I fish," said Bobby, with a wry face. "I hire a company boat and go down the river from Thursday to Sunday, and the amiable Dormer goes with me—if you can spare us both."

"You blazing young fool!" said Revere, but his heart was full of much more pleasant words.

Bobby, the captain of a dhoni, with Private Dormer for mate, dropped down the river on Thursday morning—the private at the bow, the subaltern at the helm. The private glared uneasily at the subaltern, who respected the reserve of the private.

After six hours, Dormer paced to the stern, saluted and said: "Beg y' pardon, sir, but was you ever on the Durh'm Canal?"

"No," said Bobby Wick. "Come and have some tiffin."

They ate in silence. As the evening fell, Private Dormer broke forth, speaking to himself:

"Hi was on the Durh'm Canal, jes' such a night,

come next week twelve-month, a-trailin' of my toes in the water." He smoked and said no more till bedtime.

The witchery of the dawn turned the gray river reaches to purple, gold, and opal; and it was as though the lumbering dhoni crept across the splendors of a new heaven.

Private Dormer popped his head out of his blanket and gazed at the glory below and around.

"Well, damn my eyes!" said Private Dormer in an awed whisper. "This 'ere is like a bloomin' gallantry-show!" For the rest of the day he was dumb, but achieved an ensanguined filthiness through the cleaning of big fish.

The boat returned on Saturday evening. Dormer had been struggling with speech since noon. As the lines and luggage were being disembarked, he found tongue.

"Beg y' pardon, sir," he said, "but would you— would you min' shakin' 'ands with me, sir?"

"Of course not," said Bobby, and he shook accordingly. Dormer returned to barracks and Bobby to mess.

"He wanted a little quiet and some fishing, I think," said Bobby. "My aunt, but he's a filthy sort of animal! Have you ever seen him clean 'them muchly fish with 'is thumbs?'"

"Anyhow," said Revere three weeks later, "he's doing his best to keep his things clean."

When the spring died, Bobby joined in the general scramble for Hill leave, and to his surprise and delight secured three months.

"As good a boy as I want," said Revere, the admiring skipper.

"The best of the batch," said the adjutant to the colonel. "Keep back that young skrimshanker Porkiss, sir, and let Revere make him sit up."

So Bobby departed joyously to Simla Pahar with a tin box of gorgeous raiment.

"Son of Wick—old Wick, of Chota-Buldana? Ask him to dinner, dear?" said the aged men.

"What a nice boy!" said the matrons and the maids.

"First-class place, Simla. Oh, ri—ipping!" said Bobby Wick, and ordered new cord breeches on the strength of it.

"We're in a bad way," wrote Revere to Bobby at the end of two months. "Since you left, the regiment has taken to fever and is fairly rotten with it—two hundred in hospital, about a hundred in cells —drinking to keep off fever—and the companies on parade fifteen file strong at the outside. There's rather more sickness in the out-villages than I care for, but then I'm so blistered with prickly-heat that I'm ready to hang myself. What's the yarn about your mashing a Miss Haverly up there? Not serious, I hope? You're over-young to hang millstones round your neck, and the colonel will turf you out of that in double-quick time if you attempt it."

It was not the colonel that brought Bobby out of Simla, but a much more to be respected commandant. The sickness in the out-villages spread, the bazaar was put out of bounds, and then came the news that the Tail Twisters must go into camp. The message flashed to the Hill stations: "Cholera —Leave stopped—Officers recalled." Alas, for the white gloves in the neatly soldered boxes, the rides and the dances and picnics that were to be, the love half spoken, and the debt unpaid! Without demur and without question, fast as tongue could fly or pony gallop, back to their regiments and their batteries, as though they were hastening to their weddings, fled the subalterns.

Bobby received his mandate on returning from a dance at Viceregal Lodge, where he had— But only the Haverly girl knows what Bobby had said or how many waltzes he had claimed for the next ball. Six in the morning saw Bobby at the Tonga Office in the drenching rain, the whirl of the last waltz still in his ears, and an intoxication due neither to wine nor waltzing in his brain.

"Good man!" shouted Deighton of the horse battery through the mists. "Whar you raise dat tonga? I'm coming with you. Ow! But I've a head and half. I didn't sit out all night. They say the battery's awful bad," and he hummed dolorously:

> "Leave the what at the what's-its-name,
> Leave the flock without shelter,
> Leave the corpse uninterred,
> Leave the bride at the altar!

"My faith! It'll be more bally corpse than bride, though, this journey. Jump in, Bobby, *Chalo Coachwan!*"

On the Umballa platform waited a detachment of officers discussing the latest news from the stricken cantonment, and it was here that Bobby learned the real condition of the Tail Twisters.

"They went into camp," said an elderly major recalled from the whist-tables at Mussoorie to a sickly native regiment, "they went into camp with two hundred and ten sick in carts. Two hundred and ten fever cases only, and the balance looking like so many ghosts with sore eyes. A Madras regiment could have walked through 'em!"

"But they were as fit as bedamned when I left them!" said Bobby.

"Then you'd better make them as fit as bedamned when you rejoin," said the major, brutally.

Bobby pressed his forehead against the rain-splashed window-pane as the train lumbered across the sodden Doab, and prayed for the health of the Tyneside Tail Twisters. Naini Tal had sent down her contingent with all speed; the lathering ponies of the Dalhousie Road staggered into Pathankot, taxed to the full stretch of their strength; while from cloudy Darjiling the Calcutta mail whirled up the last straggler of the little army that was to fight a fight, in which was neither medal nor honor for the winning, against an enemy none other than "the sickness that destroyeth in the noonday."

And as each man reported himself, he said: "This is a bad business," and went about his own forthwith, for every regiment and battery in the cantonment was under canvas, the sickness bearing them company.

Bobby fought his way through the rain to the Tail Twisters' temporary mess, and Revere could have fallen on the boy's neck for the joy of seeing that ugly, wholesome phiz once more.

"Keep 'em amused and interested," said Revere. "They went on the drink, poor fools, after the first two cases, and there was no improvement. Oh, it's good to have you back, Bobby! Porkiss is a—never mind."

Deighton came over from the artillery camp to attend a dreary mess dinner, and contributed to the general gloom by nearly weeping over the condition of his beloved battery. Porkiss so far forgot himself as to insinuate that the presence of the officers could do no earthly good, and that the best thing would be to send the entire regiment into hospital and "let the doctors look after them." Porkiss was demoralized with fear, nor was his peace of mind restored when Revere said, coldly:

"Oh! The sooner you go out the better, if that's your way of thinking. Any public school could send us fifty good men in your place, but it takes time, time, Porkiss, and money, and a certain amount of trouble, to make a regiment. 'Spose you're the person we go into camp for, eh?"

Whereupon Porkiss was overtaken with a great and chilly fear which a drenching in the rain did not allay, and, two days later, quitted this world for another where, men do fondly hope, allowances are made for the weakness of the flesh. The regimental sergeant-major looked wearily across the sergeants' mess tent when the news was announced.

"There goes the worst of them," he said. "It'll take the best, and then, please God, it'll stop." The sergeants were silent till one said: "It couldn't be him!" and all knew of whom Travis was thinking.

Bobby Wick stormed through the tents of his company, rallying, rebuking, mildly, as is consistent with the regulations, chaffing the faint-hearted; hauling the sound into the watery sunlight when there was a break in the weather, and bidding them to be of good cheer for their trouble was nearly at an end; scuttling on his dun pony round the outskirts of the camp and heading back men who, with the innate perversity of British soldiers, were always wandering into infected villages, or drinking deeply from rain-flooded marshes; comforting the panic-stricken with rude speech, and more than once tending the dying who had no friends—the men without "townies;" organizing, with banjos and burned cork, sing-songs which should allow the talent of the regiment full play; and generally, as he explained, "playing the giddy garden goat all round."

"You're worth half a dozen of us, Bobby," said his skipper in a moment of enthusiasm. "How the devil do you keep it up?"

Bobby made no answer, but had Revere looked into the breast-pocket of his coat he might have seen there a sheaf of badly written letters which perhaps accounted for the power that possessed the boy. A letter came to Bobby every other day. The spelling was not above reproach, but the sentiments must have been most satisfactory, for on receipt Bobby's eyes softened marvelously, and he was wont to fall into a tender abstraction for awhile ere, shaking his cropped head, he charged into his work anew.

By what power he drew after him the hearts of the roughest, and the Tail Twisters counted in their ranks some rough diamonds indeed, was a mystery to both skipper and C. O., who learned from the regimental chaplain that Bobby was considerably more in request in the hospital tents than the Reverend John Emery.

"The men seem fond of you. Are you in the hospitals much?" said the colonel, who did his daily round and ordered the men to get well with a grimness that did not cover his bitter grief.

"A little, sir," said Bobby.

"Shouldn't go there too often if I were you. They

say it's not contagious, but there's no use in running unnecessary risks. We can't afford to have you down, y'know."

Six days later, it was with the utmost difficulty that the post-runner plashed his way out to the camp with the mail-bags, for the rain was falling in torrents. Bobby received a letter, bore it off to his tent, and, the program for the next week's sing-song being satisfactorily disposed of, sat down to answer it. For an hour the unhandy pen toiled over the paper, and where sentiment rose to more than normal tide-level, Bobby Wick stuck out his tongue and breathed heavily. He was not used to letter-writing.

"Beg y' pardon, sir," said a voice at the tent door; "but Dormer's 'orrid bad, sir, an' they've taken him orf, sir."

"Damn Private Dormer and you too!" said Bobby Wick, running the blotter over the half-finished letter. "Tell him I'll come in the morning."

" 'E's awful bad, sir," said the voice, hesitatingly. There was an undecided squelching of heavy boots.

"Well?" said Bobby, impatiently.

"Excusin' 'imself before'and for takin' the liberty, 'e says it would be a comfort for to assist 'im, sir, if——"

"*Tattoo lao!* Here, come in out of the rain till I'm ready. What blasted nuisances you are! That's brandy. Drink some. You want it. Hang on to my stirrup and tell me if I go too fast."

Strengthened by a four-finger "nip," which he absorbed without a wink, the hospital orderly kept up with the slipping, mud-stained, and very disgusted pony as it shambled to the hospital tent.

Private Dormer was certainly " 'orrid bad." He had all but reached the stage of collapse and was not pleasant to look upon.

"What's this, Dormer?" said Bobby, bending over the man. "You're not going out this time. You've got to come fishing with me once or twice more yet."

The blue lips parted and in the ghost of a whisper said: "Beg y' pardon, sir, disturbin' of you now, but would you min' 'oldin' my 'and, sir?"

Bobby sat on the side of the bed, and the icy cold hand closed on his own like a vise, forcing a lady's ring which was on the little finger deep into the flesh. Bobby set his lips and waited, the water dripping from the hem of his trousers. An hour passed and the grasp of the hand did not relax, nor did the expression of the drawn face change. Bobby with infinite craft lighted himself a cheroot with the left hand, his right arm was numbed to the elbow, and resigned himself to a night of pain.

Dawn showed a very white-faced subaltern sitting on the side of a sick man's cot, and a doctor in the door-way using language unfit for publication.

"Have you been here all night, you young ass?" said the doctor.

"There or thereabouts," said Bobby, ruefully. "He's frozen on to me."

Dormer's mouth shut with a click. He turned his

head and sighed. The clinging hand opened, and Bobby's arm fell useless at his side.

"He'll do," said the doctor, quietly. "It must have been a toss-up all through the night. Think you're to be congratulated on this case."

"Oh, bosh!" said Bobby. "I thought the man had gone out long ago—only—only I didn't care to take my hand away. Rub my arm down, there's a good chap. What a grip the brute has! I'm chilled to the marrow!" He passed out of the tent shivering.

Private Dormer was allowed to celebrate his repulse of death by strong waters. Four days later, he sat on the side of his cot and said to the patients, mildly: "I'd 'a' liken to 'a' spoken to 'im—so I should."

But at that time Bobby was reading yet another letter—he had the most persistent correspondent of any man in camp—and was even then about to write that the sickness had abated, and in another week at the outside would be gone. He did not intend to say that the chill of a sick man's hand seemed to have struck into the heart whose capacities for affection he dwelt on at such length. He did not intend to inclose the illustrated program of the forthcoming singsong whereof he was not a little proud. He also intended to write on many other matters which do not concern us, and doubtless would have done so but for the slight feverish headache which made him dull and unresponsive at mess.

"You are overdoing it, Bobby," said his skipper; "'might give the rest of us credit of doing a little work. You go on as if you were the whole mess rolled into one. Take it easy."

"I will," said Bobby. "I'm feeling done up, somehow." Revere looked at him anxiously and said nothing. There was a flickering of lanterns about the camp that night, and a rumor that brought men out of their cots to the tent doors, a paddling of the naked feet of doolie-bearers and the rush of a galloping horse.

"Wot's up?" asked twenty tents; and through twenty tents ran the answer: "Wick, 'e's down."

They brought the news to Revere and he groaned. "Any one but Bobby and I shouldn't have cared! The Sergeant-Major was right."

"Not going out this journey," gasped Bobby, as he was lifted from the doolie. "Not going out this journey." Then with an air of supreme conviction: "I can't you see."

"Not if I can do anything!" said the surgeon-major, who had hastened over from the mess where he had been dining.

He and the regimental surgeon fought together with death for the life of Bobby Wick. Their ministrations were interrupted by a hairy apparition in a blue-gray dressing gown who stared in round-eyed horror at the bed and cried: "Ow, my Gawd! It can't be 'im!" until an indignant hospital orderly whisked him away.

If the care of man and desire to live could have done aught, Bobby would have been saved. As it was, he made a fight of three days, and the surgeon-major's brow uncreased. "We'll save him yet," he said; and the surgeon, who, though he ranked with the captain, had a very youthful heart, went out upon the word and pranced joyously in the mud.

"Not going out this journey," whispered Bobby Wick, gallantly, at the end of the third day.

"Bravo!" said the surgeon-major. "That's the way to look at it, Bobby."

As evening fell a gray shade gathered round Bobby's mouth, and he turned his face to the tent wall wearily. The surgeon-major frowned.

"I'm awfully tired," said Bobby, very faintly. "What's the use of bothering me with medicine? I—don't—want—it. Let me alone."

The desire for life had departed, and Bobby was content to drift away on the easy tide of death.

"It's no good," said the surgeon-major. "He doesn't want to live. He's meeting it, poor child." And he blew his nose.

Half a mile away the regimental band was playing the overture to the sing-song, for the men had been told that Bobby was out of danger. The clash of the brass and the wail of the horns reached Bobby's ears.

> "Is there a single joy or pain,
>   That I should never know—ow?

> You do not love me, 'tis in vain,
>   Bid me good-bye and go!"

An expression of hopeless irritation crossed the boy's face, and he tried to shake his head.

The surgeon-major bent down. "What is it, Bobby?"

"Not that waltz," muttered Bobby. "That's our own—our very ownest own. . . . Mummy dear."

With this oracular sentence he sunk into the stupor that gave place to death early next morning.

Revere, his eyes red at the rims and his nose very white, went into Bobby's tent to write a letter to Papa Wick, which should bow the white head of the ex-commissioner of Chota-Buldana in the keenest sorrow of his life. Bobby's little store of papers lay in confusion on the table, and among them a half-finished letter. The last sentence ran: "So you see, darling, there is really no fear, because as long as I know you care for me and I care for you, nothing can touch me."

Revere stayed in the tent for an hour. When he came out, his eyes were redder than ever.

*   *   *   *   *   *   *

Private Conklin sat on a turned-down bucket, and listened to a not unfamiliar tune. Private Conklin was a convalescent and should have been tenderly treated.

"Ho!" said Private Conklin. "There's another bloomin' orf'cer da—ed."

The bucket shot from under him, and his eyes filled with a smithyful of sparks. A tall man in a blue-gray bed-gown was regarding him with deep disfavor.

"You ought to take shame for yourself, Conky! Orf'cer? Bloomin' orf'cer? I'll learn you to mis-name the likes of 'im. Hangel! Bloomin' hangel! That's wot 'e is!"

And the hospital orderly was so satisfied with the justice of the punishment that he did not even order Private Dormer back to his cot.

IN THE MATTER
OF A PRIVATE

IN THE MATTER OF A PRIVATE

Hurrah! hurrah! a soldier's life for me!
Shout, boys, shout! for it makes you jolly and free.
                                        —*The Ramrod Corps.*

PEOPLE who have seen, state that one of the quaintest spectacles of human frailty is an outbreak of hysterics in a girls' school. It starts without warning, generally on a hot afternoon, among the elder pupils. A girl giggles till the giggle gets beyond control. Then she throws up her head, and cries: "Honk, honk, honk," like a wild goose, and tears mix with the laughter. If the mistress be wise, she will say something severe at this point to check matters. If she be tender-hearted, and send for a drink of water, the chances are largely in favor of another girl laughing at the afflicted one and herself collapsing. Thus the trouble spreads, and may end in half of what answers to the lower sixth of a boys' school rocking and whooping together. Given a week of warm weather, two stately promenades per diem, a heavy mutton and rice meal in the middle of the day, a certain amount of nagging from the teachers, and a few other things, some really amazing effects can be secured. At least, this is what folk say who have had experience.

Now, the mother superior of a convent and the colonel of a British infantry regiment would be justly shocked at any comparison being made between their respective charges. But it is a fact that, under certain circumstances, Thomas in bulk can be worked up into ditthering, rippling hysteria. He does not weep, but he shows his trouble unmistakably, and the consequences get into the newspapers, and all the good and virtuous people who hardly know a Martini from a Snider say: "Take away the brute's ammunition!"

Thomas isn't a brute, and his business, which is to look after the virtuous people, demands that he shall have his ammunition to his hand. He doesn't wear silk stockings, and he really ought to be supplied with a new adjective to help him to express his opinions: but, for all that, he is a great man. If you call him "the heroic defender of the national honor" one day, and "a brutal and licentious soldiery" the next, you naturally bewilder him, and he looks upon you with suspicion. There is nobody to speak for Thomas except people who have theories to work off on him; and nobody understands Thomas except Thomas, and he does not know what is the matter with himself.

That is the prologue. This is the story:

Corporal Slane was engaged to be married to Miss Jhansi McKenna, whose history is well known in the regiment and elsewhere. He had secured his colonel's leave, and, being popular with the men, every arrangement had been made to give the wedding

what Private Ortheris called "eeklar." It fell in
the heart of the hot weather, and, after the wedding, Slane was going up to the hills with the bride.
None the less, Slane's grievance was that the affair
would be only a hired carriage wedding, and he felt
that the "eeklar" of that was meager. Miss Mc-
Kenna did not care so much. The sergeant's wife
was helping her to make her wedding-dress, and
she was very busy. Slane was, just then, the only
moderately contented man in barracks. All the rest
were more or less miserable.

And they had so much to make them happy, too!
All their work was over at eight in the morning, and
for the rest of the day they could lie on their backs
and smoke canteen plug and swear at the punkah-
coolies. They enjoyed a fine, full flesh meal in the
middle of the day, and then threw themselves down
on their cots and sweated and slept till it was cool
enough to go out with their "towny," whose vocab-
ulary contained less than six hundred words, and
the adjective, and whose views on every conceivable
question they had heard many months before.

There was the canteen of course, and there was
the temperance-room with the second-hand papers
in it; but a man of any profession can not read for
eight hours a day in a temperature of ninety-six or
ninety-eight degrees in the shade, running up sometimes to one hundred and three degrees at midnight.
Very few men, even though they get a pannikin of
flat, stale, muddy beer and hide it under their cots,

can continue drinking for six hours a day. One man
tried, but he died, and nearly the whole regiment
went to his funeral because it gave them something
to do. It was too early for the modified excitement
of fever or cholera. The men could only wait and
wait and wait, and watch the shadow of the barrack
creeping across the blinding white dust. That was
a gay life!

They lounged about cantonments—it was too hot
for any sort of game, and almost too hot for vice—
and fuddled themselves in the evening, and filled
themselves to distension with the healthy nitrogen-
ous food provided for them, and the more they
stoked the less exercise they took and more explosive
they grew. Then the tempers began to wear away,
and men fell a-brooding over insults real or imag-
inary. They had nothing else to think of. The tone
of the "repartees" changed, and instead of saying,
light-heartedly, "I'll knock your silly face in," men
grew laboriously polite and hinted that the cantonments were not big enough for themselves and their
enemy, and that there would be more space for one of
the two in a place which it is not polite to mention.

It may have been the devil who arranged the
thing, but the fact of the case is that Losson had for
a long time been worrying Simmons in an aimless
way. It gave him occupation. The two men had
their cots side by side, and would sometimes spend a
long afternoon swearing at each other; but Simmons
was afraid of Losson and dared not challenge him to

a fight. He thought over the words in the hot still nights, and half the hate he felt toward Losson he vented on the wretched punkah-coolie.

Losson bought a parrot in the bazaar, and put it into a little cage, and lowered the cage into the cool darkness of a well, and sat on the well-curb, shouting bad language down to the parrot. He taught it to say: "Simmons, ye *so-oor*," which means swine, and several other things entirely unfit for publication. He was a big gross man, and he shook like jelly when the parrot caught the sentence correctly. Simmons, however, shook with rage, for all the room were laughing at him—the parrot was such a disreputable puff of green feathers and looked so human when it chattered. Losson used to sit, swinging his fat legs, on the side of the cot, and ask the parrot what it thought of Simmons. The parrot would answer: "Simmons, ye *so-oor*." "Good boy," Losson used to say, scratching the parrot's head; "ye 'ear that, Sim?" And Simmons used to turn over on his stomach and make answer: "I 'ear. Take 'eed you don't 'ear something one of these days."

In the restless nights, after he had been asleep all day, fits of blind rage came upon Simmons and held him till he trembled all over, while he thought in how many different ways he would slay Losson. Sometimes he would picture himself trampling the life out of the man, with heavy ammunition boots, and at others smashing in his face with the butt, and at others jumping on his shoulders and dragging the head back till the neckbone cracked. Then his mouth would feel hot and fevered, and he would reach out for another sup of the beer in the pannikin.

But the fancy that came to him most frequently and stayed with him longest was one connected with the great roll of fat under Losson's right ear. He noticed it first on a moonlight night, and thereafter it was always before his eyes. It was a fascinating roll of fat. A man could get his hand upon it and tear away one side of the neck; or he could place the muzzle of a rifle on it and blow away all the head in a flash. Losson had no right to be sleek and contented and well-to-do, when he, Simmons, was the butt of the room. Some day, perhaps, he would show those who laughed at the "Simmons, ye *so-oor*" joke, that he was as good as the rest, and held a man's life in the crook of his forefinger. When Losson snored, Simmons hated him more bitterly than ever. Why should Losson be able to sleep when Simmons had to stay awake hour after hour, tossing and turning on the tapes, with the dull pain gnawing into his right side and his head throbbing and aching after canteen? He thought over this for many nights, and the world became unprofitable to him. He even blunted his naturally fine appetite with beer and tobacco; and all the while the parrot talked at and made a mock of him.

The heat continued and the tempers wore away more quickly than before. A sergeant's wife died of heat-apoplexy in the night, and the rumor ran abroad that it was cholera. Men rejoiced openly, hoping that it would spread and send them into camp. But that was a false alarm.

It was late on a Tuesday evening, and the men were waiting in the deep double verandas for "last posts," when Simmons went to the box at the foot of his bed, took out his pipe, and slammed the lid down with a bang that echoed through the deserted barrack like the crack of a rifle. Ordinarily speaking, the men would have taken no notice; but their nerves were fretted to fiddle-strings. They jumped up, and three or four clattered into the barrack-room only to find Simmons kneeling by his box.

"Ow! It's you, is it?" they said, and laughed foolishly; "we thought 'twas——"

Simmons rose slowly. If the accident had so shaken his fellows, what would not the reality do?

"You thought it was—did you? And what makes you think?" he said, lashing himself into madness as he went on; "to hell with your thinking, ye dirty spies."

"Simmons, ye *so-oor,*" chuckled the parrot in the veranda, sleepily, recognizing a well-known voice. And that was absolutely all.

The tension snapped. Simmons fell back on the arm-rack deliberately—the men were at the far end of the room—and took out his rifle and packet of ammunition. "'Don't go playing the goat, Sim!'" said Losson; "put it down," but there was a quaver in his voice. Another man stopped, slipped his boot and hurled it at Simmons's head. The prompt answer was a shot which, fired at random, found its billet in Losson's throat. Losson fell forward without a word, and the others scattered.

"You thought it was!" yelled Simmons. "You're drivin' me to it!   I tell you you're drivin' me to it! Get up, Losson, an' don't lie shammin' there—you an' your blasted parrit that druv me to it!"

But there was an unaffected reality about Losson's pose that showed Simmons what he had done. The men were still clamoring in the veranda.   Simmons appropriated two more packets of ammunition and ran into the moonlight muttering: "I'll make a night of it.   Thirty roun's, an' the last for myself. Take you that, you dogs!"

He dropped on one knee and fired into the brown of the men in the veranda, but the bullet flew high, and landed in the brickwork with a vicious "phwit" that made some of the younger men turn pale. It is, as musketry theorists observe, one thing to fire and another to be fired at.

Then the instinct of the chase flared up. The news spread from barrack to barrack, and the men doubled out intent on the capture of Simmons, the wild beast, who was heading for the cavalry parade-ground, stopping now and again to send a shot and a curse in the direction of his pursuers.

"I'll learn you to spy on me!" he shouted; "I'll learn you to give me dorg's names!   Come on the 'ole lot o' you! Colonel John Anthony Deever, C. B.!"

—he turned toward the infantry mess and shook his rifle—"you think yourself the devil of a man—but I tell you that if you put your ugly old carcass outside o' that door, I'll make you the poorest-lookin' man in the army. Come out, Colonel John Anthony Deever, C. B.! Come out and see me practiss on the rainge. I'm the crack shot of the 'ole bloomin' battalion." In proof of which statement Simmons fired at the lighted windows of the mess-house.

"Private Simmons, E Comp'ny, on the cavalry p'rade-ground, sir, with thirty rounds," said a sergeant, breathlessly, to the colonel. "Shootin' right and lef' sir. Shot Private Losson. What's to be done, sir?"

Colonel John Anthony Deever, C. B., sallied out, only to be saluted by a spurt of dust at his feet.

"Pull up!" said the second in command; "I don't want my step in that way, colonel. He's as dangerous as a mad dog!"

"Shoot him like one, then," said the colonel, bitterly, "if he won't take his chance. My regiment, too! If it had been the Towheads I could have understood."

Private Simmons had occupied a strong position near a well on the edge of the parade-ground, and was defying the regiment to come on. The regiment was not anxious to comply with the request, for there is small honor in being shot by a fellow private. Only Corporal Slane, rifle in hand, threw himself down on the ground, and wormed his way toward the well.

"Don't shoot," said he to the men round him; "like as not you'll 'it me. I'll catch the beggar livin'!"

Simmons ceased shouting for awhile, and the noise of trap-wheels could be heard across the plain. Major Oldyne, commanding the horse battery, was coming back from a dinner in the civil lines; was driving after his usual custom—that is to say, as fast as the horse could go.

"A orf'cer! A blooming spangled orf'cer!" shrieked Simmons; "I'll make a scarecrow of that orf'cer!" The trap stopped.

"What's this?" demanded the major of gunners. "You there, drop your rifle!"

"Why, it's Jerry Blazes! I ain't got no quarrel with you, Jerry Blazes. Pass, fren', an' all's well!"

But Jerry Blazes had not the faintest intention of passing a dangerous murderer. He was, as his adoring battery swore long and fervently, without knowledge of fear, and they were surely the best judges, for Jerry Blazes, it was notorious, had done his possible to kill a man each time the battery went out.

He walked toward Simmons, with the intention of rushing him, and knocking him down.

"Don't make me do it, sir," said Simmons; "I ain't got nothing agin you. Ah! you would?"—the major broke into a run—"Take that, then!"

The major dropped with a bullet through his shoulder, and Simmons stood over him. He had lost the satisfaction of killing Losson in the desired way; but here was a helpless body to his hand. Should he slip in another cartridge, and blow off the head, or with the butt smash in the white face? He stopped to consider, and a cry went up from the far side of the parade-ground: "He's killed Jerry Blazes!" But in the shelter of the well-pillars Simmons was safe, except when he stepped out to fire. "I'll blow your 'andsome 'ead off, Jerry Blazes," said Simmons, reflectively; "six an' three is nine an' one is ten, an' that leaves me another nineteen, an' one for myself." He tugged at the string of the second packet of ammunition. Corporal Slane crawled out of the shadow of a bank into the moonlight.

"I see you!" said Simmons; "come a bit furder on an' I'll do for you."

"I'm comin'," said Corporal Slane, briefly; "you done a bad day's work, Sim. Come out 'ere an' come back with me."

"Come to—" laughed Simmons, sending a cartridge home with his thumb. "Not before I've settled you an' Jerry Blazes."

The corporal was lying at full length in the dust of the parade-ground, a rifle under him. Some of the less cautious men in the distance shouted: "Shoot 'im! Shoot 'im, Slane!"

"You move 'and or foot, Slane," said Simmons, "an' I'll kick Jerry Blazes's 'ead in, and shoot you after."

"I ain't movin'," said the corporal, raising his

head; "you daren't 'it a man on 'is legs. Let go o'
Jerry Blazes an' come out o' that with your fists.
Come an' 'it me. You daren't, you bloomin' dog-
shooter!"

"I dare."

"You lie, you man-sticker. You sneakin', sheeny
butcher, you lie! See there!" Slane kicked the rifle
away, and stood up, in the peril of his life. "Come
on, now!"

The temptation was more than Simmons could
resist, for the corporal in his white clothes offered a
perfect mark.

"Don't misname me," shouted Simmons, firing
as he spoke. The shot missed, and the shooter,
blind with rage, threw his rifle down and rushed at
Slane from the protection of the well. Within
striking distance, he kicked savagely at Slane's
stomach, but the weedy corporal knew something
of Simmons's weakness, and knew, too, the deadly
guard for that kick. Bowing forward and drawing
up his right leg till the heel of the right foot was set
some three inches above the inside of the left knee-
cap, he met the blow standing on one leg—exactly
as Gonds stand when they meditate—and ready for
the fall that would follow. There was an oath,
the corporal fell over to his own left as shinbone
met shinbone, and the private collapsed, his right
leg broken an inch above the ankle.

"Pity you don't know that guard, Sim," said Slane,
spitting out the dust as he rose. Then raising his

voice: "Come an' take him orf. I've bruk 'is leg." This was not strictly true, for the private had accomplished his own downfall, since it is the special merit of that leg-guard that the harder the kick the greater the kicker's discomfiture.

Slane walked to Jerry Blazes and hung over him with exaggerated solicitude, while Simmons, weeping with pain, was carried away. "'Ope you ain't 'urt badly," said Slane. The major had fainted, and there was an ugly, ragged hole through the top of his arm. Slane knelt down and murmured: "S'elp me, I believe 'e's dead. Well, if that ain't my blooming luck all over!"

But the major was destined to lead his battery afield for many a day with unshaken nerve. He was removed, and nursed and petted into convalescence, while the battery discussed the wisdom of capturing Simmons, and blowing him from a gun. They idolized their major, and his reappearance on parade resulted in a scene nowhere provided for in the army regulations.

Great, too, was the glory that fell to Slane's share. The gunners would have made him drunk thrice a day for at least a fortnight. Even the colonel of his own regiment complimented him upon his coolness, and the local paper called him a hero. Which things did not puff him up. When the major proffered him money and thanks, the virtuous corporal took the one and put aside the other. But he had a request to make and prefaced it with many a "Beg y' pardon, sir." Could the major see his way to letting the Slane-McKenna wedding be adorned by the presence of four battery horses to pull a hired barouche? The major could, and so could the battery. Excessively so. It was a gorgeous wedding.

* * * * * * *

"Wot did I do it for?" said Corporal Slane. "For the 'orses, o' course. Jhansi ain't a beauty to look at, but I wasn't goin' to 'ave a hired turn-out. Jerry Blazes? If I 'adn't 'a' wanted something, Sim might ha' blowed Jerry Blazes' blooming 'ead into Hirish stew for aught I'd 'a' cared."

And they hanged Private Simmons—hanged him as high as Haman in hollow square of the regiment; and the colonel said it was drink; and the chaplain was sure it was the devil; and Simmons fancied it was both, but he didn't know, and only hoped his fate would be a warning to his companions; and half a dozen "intelligent publicists" wrote six beautiful leading articles on "The Prevalence of Crime in the Army."

But not a soul thought of comparing the "bloody-minded Simmons" to the squawking, gaping school-girl with which this story opens.

That would have been too absurd.

THE THREE MUSKETEERS

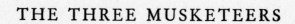

THE THREE MUSKETEERS

An' when the war began, we chased the bold Afghan,
An' we made the bloomin' Ghazi for to flee, boys O!
An' we marched into *Kabul,* and we tuk the Balar 'Issar,
An' we taught 'em to respec' the British Soldier.
Barrack Room Ballad.

MULVANEY, Ortheris and Learoyd are Privates in B Company of a Line Regiment, and personal friends of mine. Collectively, I think, but am not certain, they are the worst men in the regiment so far as genial blackguardism goes.

They told me this story, the other day, in the Umballa Refreshment Room while we were waiting for an up-train. I supplied the beer. The tale was cheap at a gallon and a half.

Of course you know Lord Benira Trig. He is a Duke, or an Earl, or something unofficial; also a Peer; also a Globe-trotter! On all three counts, as Ortheris says, " 'e didn't deserve no consideration." He was out here for three months collecting materials for a book on "Our Eastern Impedimenta," and quartering himself upon everybody, like a Cossack in evening-dress.

His particular vice—because he was a Radical, I suppose—was having garrisons turned out for his

[173]

inspection. He would then dine with the Officer commanding, and insult him, across the Mess table, about the appearance of the troops. That was Benira's way.

He turned out troops once too often. He came to Helanthami Cantonment on a Tuesday. He wished to go shopping in the bazaars on Wednesday, and he "desired" the troops to be turned out on a Thursday. On—a—Thursday! The officer Commanding could not well refuse; for Benira was a Lord. There was an indignation-meeting of subalterns in the Mess Room, to call the Colonel pet names.

'But the rale dimonstrashin," said Mulvaney, "was in B Comp'ny barrick; we three headin' it."

Mulvaney climbed on to the refreshment-bar, settled himself comfortably by the beer, and went on: —"Whin the row was at ut's foinest an' B Comp'ny was fur goin' out to murther this man Thrigg on the p'rade-groun', Learoyd here takes up his helmut an' sez—fwhat was ut ye said?"

"Ah said," said Learoyd, "gie us t' brass. Take oop a subscripshun, lads, for to put off t' p'rade, an' if t' p'rade's not put off, ah'll gie t' brass back agean. That's wot ah said. All B Coomp'ny knawed me, Ah took oop a big subscripshun—fower rupees eight annas 'twas—an' ah went oot to turn t' job over. Mulvaney an' Orth'ris coom with me."

"We three raises the Divil in couples gin'rally," explained Mulvaney.

Here Ortheris interrupted. "''Ave you read the papers?" said he.

"Sometimes," I said.

"We 'ad read the papers, an' we put hup a faked decoity, a—a sedukshun."

"Abdukshun, ye cockney," said Mulvaney.

"Abdukshun or sedukshun—no great odds. Any-'ow, we arrange to taik an' put Mister Benhira out o' the way till Thursday was hover, or 'e too busy to rux 'isself about praids. Hi was the man wot said: 'We'll make a few rupees off o' the business.' "

"We hild a Council av War," continued Mulvaney, "walkin' roun by the Artill'ry Lines. I was Prisidint, Learoyd was Minister av Finance, an' little Orth'ris here was——"

"A bloomin' Bismarck! Hi made the 'ole show pay."

"This interferin' bit av a Venira man," said Mulvaney, "did the thrick for us himself; for, on me sowl, we hadn't a notion av what was to come afther the next minut. He was shoppin' in the bazaar on fut. 'Twas drawin' dusk thin, an' we stud watchin' the little man hoppin' in an' out av the shops, thryin' to injuce the naygurs to *mallum* his *bat*. Prisintly, he sthrols up, his arrums full av thruck, an' he sez in a consiquinshal way, shticking out his little belly: —'Me good men,' sez he, 'have ye seen the Kernels b'roosh?' 'B'roosh?' says Learoyd. 'There's no b'roosh here—nobbut a *hekka*.' 'Fwhat's that?' sez Thrigg. Learoyd shows him wan down the sthreet, an' he sez:—'How thruly Orientil! I will ride on a *hekka*.' I saw thin that our Rigimintal Saint was for givin' Thrigg over to us neck an' brisket. I purshued a *hekka*, an' I sez to the dhriver-divil, I sez—'Ye black limb, there's a *Sahib* comin' for this *hekka*. He wants to go *jildi* to the Padsahi Jhil'— 'twas about tu moiles away,—'to shoot snipe—*chirria*. 'You dhrive *Fehannum ke marfik, mallum?* 'Tis no manner av *faider bukkin*' to the *Sahib*, bekaze he doesn't *samjao* your *bat*. Av he *bolos* anything, just you *choop* and *chel*. *Dekker?* Go *arsty* for the first *arder*-mile from cantonmints. Then *chel, Shaitan ke marfik,* an' the *chooper* you *choops* an' the *jilder* you *chels* the better *kooshy* will that *Sahib* be; an' here's a rupee for ye.'

"The *hekka*-man knew there was somethin' out av the common in the air. He grinned and sez:— '*Bote achee!* I goin' damn fast.' I prayed that the Kernel's b'roosh wudn't arrive till me darlin' Benira by the grace av God was undher weigh. The little man puts his thruck into the *hekka* an' scuttles in like a fat guinea-pig; niver offerin' us the price of a dhrink for our services in helpin' him home. 'He's off to the Padsahi *jhil*,' sez I to the others."

Ortheris took up the tale:—

"Jist then, little Buldoo kim up, 'oo was the son of one of the Artillery *Saises*—'e would 'av made a 'evinly newspaper-boy in London, bein' sharp and fly to all manner o' games. 'E 'ad bin watchin' us puttin' Mister Benhira into 'is temporary baroush,

an' 'e sez:—'What 'ave you been a doin' of, Sahib?'
sez 'e. Learoyd 'e caught 'im by the ear an' 'e
sez—"

"Ah says," went on Learoyd: " 'Young mon, that
mon's gooin' to have't goons out o' Thursday—*kul*—
an' thot's more work for you, young mon. Now,
sitha, tak a *tat* an' a *lookri*, an' ride tha domdest to t'
Padashi Jhil. Cotch thot there *hekka*, and tell t'
driver iv your lingo thot you've coon to tak' his place.
T' *Sahib* doesn't speak t' *bat*, an' he's a little mon.
Drive t' *hekka* into t' Padshi Jhil into t' watter.
Leave t' *Sahib* theer an' roon hoam; an' here's a
rupee for tha.' "

Then Mulvaney and Ortheris spoke together in
alternate fragments: Mulvaney leading (You must
pick out the two speakers as best you can.) "He
was a knowin' little divil was Bhuldoo,—'e sez *bote
achee* an' cuts—wid a wink in his oi—but Hi sez
there's money to be made—an' I want to see the end
av the campaign—so Hi says we'll double hout to the
Padshi Jhil—and save the little man from bein' dacoited by the murtherin' Bhuldoo—an' turn hup like
reskoors in a Ryle Victoria Theayter Melodrama—
so we doubled for the *Jhil*, an' prisintly there was the
divil of a hurroosh behind us an' three bhoys on
grasscuts' *tats* come by, pounding along for the dear
life—s'elp me Bob, hif Bhuldoo 'adn't raised a regular harmy of dacoits—to do the job in shtile. An'
we ran, an' they ran, shplittin' with laughin', till we
gets near the *jhil*—and 'ears sounds of distress float-

in' moloncally on the heavenin' hair." (Ortheris was growing poetical under the influence of the beer. The duet recommenced; Mulvaney leading again.)

"Thin we heard Bhuldoo, the dacoit, shoutin' to the *hekka* man, an' wan of the young divils brought his *lakri* down on the top av the *hekka*-cover, an' Benira Thrigg inside howled 'Murther an' Death.' Bhuldoo takes the reins and dhrives like mad for the *jhil*, havin' dishpersed the *hekka*-dhriver—'oo cum up to us an' 'e sez, sezie:—'That *Sahib's* nigh *gawbry* with funk! Wot devil's work 'ave you led me into?' 'Hall right,' sez we, 'you *puckrow* that there pony an' come along. This *Sahib's* been decoited, an' we're goin' to resky 'im!' Says the driver: 'Decoits! Wot dacoits? That's Bhuldoo the *budmash*.'—'Bhuldoo be shot!' sez we. ' 'Tis a woild dissolute Pathan frum the hills. There's about eight av 'im coercin' the *Sahib*. You remimber that an' you'll get another rupee'! Then we heard the whop-whop-whop av the *hekka* turnin' over, an' a splash av water an' the voice av Benira Thrigg callin' upon God to forgive his sins—an' Bhuldoo an' 'is friends squotterin' in the water like boys in the Serpentine."

Here the Three Musketeers retired simultaneously into the beer.

"Well? What came next?" said I.

"Fwhat nex'?" answered Mulvaney, wiping his mouth. "Wud you let three bould sodger-bhoys lave the ornamint av the House of Lords to be dhrowned an' dacoited in a *jhil?* We formed line av quarther-column an' we desinded upon the inimy. For the better part av tin minutes you could not hear yerself spake. The *tattoo* was screamin' in chune wid Benira Thrigg an' Bhuldoo's army, an' the shticks was whistlin' roun' the *hekka,* an' Orth'- ris was beatin' the *hekka*-cover wid his fistes, an' Learoyd yellin':—'Look out for their knives!' an' me cuttin' into the dark, right an' lef', dishpersin' army corps av Pathans. Holy Mother av Moses! 'twas more disp'rit than Ahmid Kheyl wid Maiwund thrown in. Afther a while Bhuldoo an' his bhoys flees. Have ye iver seen a rale live Lord thryin' to hide his nobility undher a fut an' a half av brown *jhil* wather? 'Tis the livin' image av a *bhisti's mussick* with the shivers. It tuk toime to pershuade me frind Benira he was not disimbowilled; an' more toime to get out the *hekka.* The dhriver come up afther the battle, swearin' he tuk a hand in repulsin' the inimy. Benira was sick wid the fear. We escort- ed him back, very slow, to cantonmints, for that an' the chill to soak into him. It suk! Glory be to the Rigimintil Saint, but it suk to the marrow av Lord Benira Thrigg!"

Here Ortheris, slowly, with immense pride:— "'E sez:—'You har my noble preservers,' sez 'e. 'You har a honor to the British Harmy,' sez 'e. With that 'e describes the hawful band of dacoits wot set on 'im. There was about forty of 'em an' 'e was hoverpowered by numbers, so 'e was; but 'e

never lost 'is presence of mind, so 'e didn't. 'E guv
the *hekka*-driver five rupees for 'is noble hassistance,
an' 'e said 'e would see to us after 'e 'ad spoken to
the Kernul. For we was a honor to the Regiment,
we was."

"An' we three," said Mulvaney, with a seraphic
smile, "have dhrawn the par-ti-cu-lar attinshin av
Bobs Bahadur more than wanst. But he's a rale
good little man is Bobs. Go on, Orth'ris, me son."

"Then we leaves 'im at the Kernul's 'ouse, werry
sick, an' we cuts over to B Comp'ny barrick an' we
sez we 'ave saved Benira from a bloody doom, an'
the chances was agin there bein' p'raid on Thursday.
About ten minutes later come three envelicks, one
for each of us. S'elp me Bob, if the old bloke 'adn't
guv us a fiver apiece—sixty-four dibs in the bazar!
On Thursday 'e was in 'orspital recoverin' from 'is
sanguinary encounter with a gang of Pathans, an' B
Comp'ny was drinkin' 'emselves inter clink by
squads. So there never was no Thursday p'raid.
But the Kernul, when 'e 'eard of our galliant con-
duct, 'e sez:—'Hi know there's been some deviltry
somewheres,' sez 'e, 'but hi can't bring it 'ome to
you three.' "

"An' my privit impresshin is," said Mulvaney,
getting off the bar and turning his glass upside down,
"that, av they had known they wudn't have brought
ut home. 'Tis flyin' in the face, firstly av Nature,
second, av the Rig'lations, an' third, the will av Terrence Mulvaney, to hold p'rades av Thursdays."

"Good, ma son!" said Learoyd; "but, young mon, what's t' notebook for?"

"Let be," said Mulvaney; "this time next month we're in the *sherapis*. 'Tis immortial fame the gentleman's goin' to give us. But kape it dhark till we're out av the range av me little frind Bobs Bahadur."

And I have obeyed Mulvaney's order.

THE TAKING OF
LUNGTUNGPEN

THE TAKING OF LUNGTUNGPEN

> So we loosed a bloomin' volley,
>   An' we made the beggars cut,
>   An' when our pouch was emptied out,
>   We used the bloomin' butt,
>   Ho! My!
>   Don't yer come anigh,
> When Tommy is a playin' with the baynit an' the butt.
>   *Barrack Room Ballad.*

MY friend Private Mulvaney told me this, sitting on the parapet of the road to Dagshai, when we were hunting butterflies together. He had theories about the Army, and colored clay pipes perfectly. He said that the young soldier is the best to work with, "on account av the surpassing innocinse av the child."

"Now, listen!" said Mulvaney, throwing himself full length on the wall in the sun. "I'm a born scutt av the barrick-room! The Army's mate an' drunk to me' bekaze I'm wan av the few that can't quit ut. I've put in sivinteen years, an' the pipeclay's in the marrow av me. Av I cud have kept out av wan big dhrink a month, I wud have been a Hon'ry Lift'nint by this time—a nuisaice to my betthers, a laughin'-shtock to my equils, an' a curse to mesilf. Bein' fwhat I am, Private Mulvaney, wid no goodconduc' pay an' a devourin' thirst. Always barrin' me little frind Bobs Bahadur, I know as much about the Army as most men."

I said something here.

"Wolseley be shot! Betune you an' me an' that butterfly net, he's a ramblin' inccherint sort av a divil, wid wan oi on the Quane an' the Coort, an' the other on his blessed silf—everlastin'ly playing Saysar an' Alexandrier rowled into a lump. Now Bobs is a sinsible little man. Wid Bobs an' a few three-year-olds, I'd swape any army av the earth into a *jhairun*, an' throw it away aftherwards. Faith, I'm not jokin'! 'Tis the bhoys—the raw bhoys— that don't know fwhat a bullet manes, an' wudn't care av they did—that dhu the work. They're crammed wid bullmate till they fairly ramps wid good livin'; and thin, av they don't fight, they blow each other's hids off. 'Tis the trut' I'm tellin' you. They shud be kept on *dal-bhat* an' *kijri* in the hot weather; but there'd be a mut'ny av 'twas done.

"Did ye iver hear how Privit Mulvaney tuk the town av Lungtungpen? I thought not! 'Twas the Lift'nint got thet credit; but 'twas me planned the schame. A little before I was inviladed from Burma, me an' four an' twenty young wans undher a Lift'- nint Brabenose, was ruinin' our dijeshins thryin' to catch dacoits. An' such double-ended divils I niver knew! 'Tis only a *dah* an' a Snider that makes a decoit. Widout thim, he's a paceful cultivator, an' felony for to shoot. We hunted an' we hunted, an' tuk fever an' elephants now an' again; but no dacoits. Evenshually, we *puckarowed* wan man. 'Trate him tinderly,' sez the Lift'nint. So I tuk him away into the jungle, wid the Burmese Interprut'r an' my clanin'-rod. Sez I to the man:—'My paceful squireen,' sez I, 'you shquot on your hunkers an' dimonstrate to my frind here, where your frinds are whin they're at home?' Wid that I introjuced him to the clanin'-rod, and he comminst to jabber; the Interprut'r interprutin' in betweens, an' me helpin' the Intilligince Departmint wid my clanin-rod whin the man misremembered.

"Prisintly, I lcarnt that, acrost the river, about nine miles away, was a town just *dhrippin'* wid dahs, an' bohs an' arrows, an' dacoits, an' elephints, an' *jingles*. 'Good!' sez I. 'This office will now close!'

"That night, I went to th' Lift'nint an' communicates my information. I never thought much of Lift'nint Brazenose till that night. He was shtiff wid books an' the-ouries, an' all manner av thrimmin's no manner av use. 'Town did ye say?' sez he. 'Accordin' to the-ouries av War, we shud wait for reinforcemints.' 'Faith!' thinks I, 'we'd betther dig our graves thin'; for the nearest throops was up to their shtocks in the marshes out Mimbu way. 'But,' says the Lift'nint, 'since 'tis a speshil case, I'll make an excepshin. We'll visit this Lungtungpen tonight.'

'The bhoys was fairly woild wid deloight whin I tould 'em; an' by this an' that, they wint through the jungle like buck-rabbits.   About midnight we come to the shtrame which I had clane forgot to min-shin to my orficer.   I was on, ahead, wid four bhoys, an' I thought that the Lift'nint might want to the-ourize.   'Shtrip, bhoys!' sez I.   'Shtrip to the buff, an' shwim in where glory waits!'   'But I can't shwim!' sez two av thim.   'To think I should live to hear that from a bhoy wid a board-school eduka-shin!' sez I.   'Take a lump av thimber, an' me an' Conolly here will ferry ye over, ye yong ladies!'

"We got an ould tree-trunk, an' pushed off wid the kits an' the rifles on it.   The night was chokin' dhark, an' just as we was fairly embarked, I heard the Lift-nint behind av me callin' out.   'There's a bit av a *nullah* here, Sorr,' sez I, 'but I can feel the bottom already.'   So I cud, for I was not a yard from the bank.

"'Bit av a *nullah!*   Bit av an eshtuary!' sez the Lift'nint.   'Go on, ye mad Irishman!   Shtrip, bhoys!'   I heard him laugh; an' the bhoys begun shtrippin' an' rollin' a log into the wather to put their kits on.   So me an' Conolly shtruck out through the warm wather wid our log, an' the rest come on behind.

'That shtrame was miles woide!   Orth'ris, on the rear-rank log, whispers we had got into the Thames below Sheerness by mistake.   'Kape on shwimmin', ye little blayguard,' says I, 'an' don't go pokin' your dirty jokes at the Irriwaddy.'   'Silence, men!' sings out the Lift-nint. So we shwum on into the black dhark, wid our chests on the logs, trustin' in the Saints an' the luck av the British Army.

"Evenshually, we hit ground—a bit of sand—an' a man. I put my heel on the back av him. He skreeched an' ran.

"'Now we've done it!' sez Lift-nint Brazenose. 'Where the Devil is Lungtungpen?' There was about a minute and a half to wait. The bhoys laid hold av their rifles an' some thried to put their belts on; we was marchin' wid fixed baynits av coorse. Thin we knew where Lungtungpen was; for we had hit the river-wall av it in the dark, an' the whole town blazed wid thim messin *jingles* an' Sniders like a cat's back on a frosty night. They was firin' all ways at wanst; but over our hids into the shtrame.

"'Have you got your rifles?' sez Brazenose. 'Got 'em!' sez Orth'ris, 'I've got that thief Mulvaney's for all my back pay, an' she'll kick my heart sick wid that blunderin' long shtock av hers.' 'Go on!' yells Brazenose, whippin' his sword out. 'Go on an' take the town! An' the Lord have mercy on our sowls!'

"Thin the bhoys gave wan divastatin' howl, an' pranced into the dhark, feelin' for the town, an' blindin' an' stiffin' like Cavalry Ridin' Masters whin the grass pricked their bare legs. I hammered wid the butt at some bamboo thing that felt awake, an' the rest come and hammered contagious, while the *jingles* was jingling, an' feroshus yells from inside was shplittin' our ears. We was too close under the wall for thim to hurt us.

"Evenshually, the thing, whatever ut was, bruk; an' the six and twinty av us tumbled, wan afther the other, naked as we was borrun, into the town of Lungtungpen. There was a *melly* av a sumpshus kind for a whoile; but whether they tuk us, all white an' wet, for a new breed av devil, or a new kind of dacoit, I don't know. They ran as though we was both, an' we wint into thim, baynit an' butt, shriekin' wid laughin'. There was torches in the shtreets, an' I saw little Orth'ris rubbin' his showlder ivry time he loosed my long-shtock Martini; an' Brazenose walkin' into the gang wid his sword, like Diarmid av the Golden Collar—barring he hadn't a stitch of clothin' on him. We diskivered elephints wid de-coits under their bellies, an', what wid wan thing an' another, we was busy till mornin' takin' posses-sion av the town of Lungtungpen.

"Thin we halted an' formed up, the wimmen howlin' in the houses an' Lift'nint Brazenose blushin' pink in the light av the mornin' sun. 'Twas the most ondasint p'rade I iver tuk a hand in. Foive and twenty privits an' a orf'cer av the line in review ordher, an' not as much as wud dust a fife betune 'em all in the way of clothin'! Eight of us had their belts an' pouches on; but the rest had gone in wid a handful of cartridges an' the skin God gave him. They was as nakid as Vanus.

" 'Number off from the right!' sez the Lift'nint. 'Odd numbers fall out to dress; even numbers pathrol the town till relieved by the dressing party.' Let me tell you, pathrolin' a town wid nothing on is an expayrience. I pathroled for ten minutes, an' begad, before 'twas over, I blushed. The women laughed so. I niver blushed before or since; but I blushed all over my carkiss thin. Orth'ris didn't pathrol. He sez only:—'Portsmith Barricks an' the 'Ard av a Sunday!' Thin he lay down an' rowled anyways wid laughin'.

"When we was all dhressed, we counted the dead —sivinty-foive dacoits besides wounded. We tuk five elephints, a hunder' an' sivinty Sniders, two hunder' dahs, and a lot av other burglarious thruck. Not a man av us was hurt—excep' maybe the Lift'-nint, an' he from the shock to his dasincy.

"The Headman av Lungtungpen, who surrinder'd himself, asked the Interprut'r.—'Av the English fight like that wid their clo'es off, what in the wur-ruld do they do wid their clo'es on?' Orth'ris began rowlin' his eyes an' crackin' his fingers an' dancin' a step-dance for to impress the Headman. He ran to his house; an' we spint the rest av the day carryin' the Lift'nint on our showlthers round the town, an' playin' wid the Burmese babies—fat, little, brown little devils, as pretty as pictures.

"Win I was inviladed for the Dysent'ry to India, I sez to the Lift'nint:—'Sirr,' sez I, 'you've the

makin's in you av a great man; but, av you'll let an
ould sodger spake, you're too fond of the-ourizin'.
He shuk hands wid me and sez:—'Hit high, hit
low, there's no plasin' you, Mulvaney. You've seen
me waltzin' through Lungtungpen like a Red Injun
widout war-paint, an' you say I'm too fond av the-
ourizin'?' 'Sorr,' sez I, for I loved the bhoy; 'I
wud waltz wid you in that condishin through Hell,
an' so wud the rest av the men!' Thin I wint down-
shtrame in the flat an' left him my blessin'. May
the Saints carry ut where ut shud go, for he was a
fine upstandin' young orficer.

"To reshume! Fwhat I've said jist shows the
use av three-year-olds. Wud fifty seasoned sodgers
have taken Lungtungpen in the dhark that way?
No! They'd know the risk av fever an' chill. Let
alone the shootin'. Two hundher' might have done
ut. But the three-year-olds know little an' care less;
an' where there's no fear, there's no danger. Catch
thim young, feed thim high, an' by the honor av
that great, little man Bobs, behind a good orficer
'tisn't only dacoits they'd smash wid their clo'es off
—'tis Con-ti-nental Ar-r-r-mies! They tuk Lungtungpen nakid; an' they'd take St. Pethersburg in
their dhrawers! Begad, they would that!

"Here's your pipe, Sorr! Shmoke her tinderly
wid honey-dew, afther letting the reek av the Canteen plug die away. But 'tis no good, thanks to you
all the same, fillin' my pouch wid your chopped

bhoosa.   Canteen baccy's like the Army.   It shpoils a man's taste for moilder things."

So saying, Mulvaney took up his butterfly-net, and marched to barracks.

THE DAUGHTER OF THE
REGIMENT

THE DAUGHTER OF THE REGIMENT

Jain 'Ardin' was a Sarjint's wife,
  A Sarjint's wife wus she.
She married of 'im in Orldershort
  An' comed acrost the sea.
(*Chorus*) 'Ave you never 'eard tell o' Jain 'Ardin?
                     Jain 'Ardin'?
                     Jain 'Ardin'?
  'Ave you never 'eard tell o' Jain 'Ardin'?
The pride o' the Compan*ee*?
Old Barrack Room Ballad.

"A GENTLEMAN who doesn't know the Circassian Circle ought not to stand up for it—puttin' everybody out." That was what Miss McKenna said, and the Sergeant who was my *vis-a-vis* looked the same thing. I was afraid of Miss McKenna. She was six feet high, all yellow freckles and red hair, and was simply clad in white satin shoes, a pink muslin dress, an apple-green stuff sash, and black silk gloves, with yellow roses in her hair. Wherefore I fled from Miss McKenna and sought my friend Private Mulvaney who was at the cant—refreshment-table.

"So you've been dancin' with little Jhansi McKenna, Sorr—she that's goin' to marry Corp'ril Slane? Whin you next conversh wid your lorruds an' your ladies, tell thim you've danced wid little Jhansi. 'Tis a thing to be proud av."

But I wasn't proud. I was humble. I saw a story in Private Mulvaney's eye; and, besides, if he stayed too long at the bar, he would, I knew, qualify for more pack-drill. Now to meet an esteemed friend doing pack-drill outside the guard-room, is embarrassing, especially if you happen to be walking with his Commanding Officer.

"Come on to the parade-ground, Mulvaney, it's cooler there, and tell me about Miss McKenna. What is she, and who is she, and why is she called 'Jhansi'?"

"D'ye mane to say you've never heard av Ould Pummeloe's daughter? An' you thinkin' you know things! I'm wid ye in a minut' whin me poipe's lit."

We came out under the stars. Mulvaney sat down on one of the artillery bridges, and began in the usual way: his pipe between his teeth, his big hands clasped and dropped between his knees, and his cap well on the back of his head:

"Whin Mrs. Mulvaney, that is, was Miss Chad that was, you were a dale younger than you are now, an' the Army was dif'rint in sev'ril e-sen-shuls. Bhoys have no call for to marry nowadays, an' that's why the Army has so few rale, good, honust, swearin', strapagin', tinder-hearted, heavy-futted wives as ut used to hav whin I was a Corp'ril. I was rejuced afterwards—but no matther—I was a Corp'ril wanst.

In thim times, a man lived an' died wid his rigiment; an' by natur', he married whin he was a man. Whin I was Corp'ril—Mother av Hivin, how the rigimint has died an' been borrun since that day! —my Color-Sar'jint was Ould McKenna, an' a married man tu. An' his woife—his first woife, for he married three times did McKenna—was Bridget McKenna, from Portarlington, like mesilf. I've misremembered fwhat her first name was; but in B Comp'ny we called her 'Ould Pummeloe' by reasan av her figure, which was entirely cir-cum-fe-renshil. Like the big dhrum! Now that woman— God rock her sowl to rest in glory!—was for everlastin' havin' childher: an' McKenna, whin the fifth or sixth come squallin' on to the musther-roll, swore he wud number them off in future. But Ould Pummeloe she prayed av him to christen thim after the names of the stations they was borrun in. So there was Colaba McKenna, an' Muttra McKenna, an' a whole Presidincy av other McKennas, an' little Jhansi, dancin' over yonder. Whin the children wasn't bornin', they was dying; for, av our childer die like sheep in these days, they died like flies thin. I lost me own little Shad—but no matther. 'Tis long ago, and Mrs. Mulvaney niver had another.

"I'm digresshin. Wan divil's hot summer there come an order from some mad ijjit, whose name I misremember, for the rigimint to go up-country. May be they wanted to know how the new rail carried throops. They knew! On me sowl, they knew before they was done! Ould Pummeloe had just buried Muttra McKenna; an' the season bein' onwholesim, only little Jhansi McKenna, who was four year ould thin, was left on hand.

"Five children gone in fourteen months. 'Twas harrd, wasn't ut?

"So we wint up to our new station in that blazin' heat—may the curse av Saint Lawrence conshume the man who gave the ordher! Will I ivir forget that move? They gave us two wake thrains to the rigimint; an' we was eight hundher' and sivinty strong. There was A. B. C. an' D. Companies in the secon' thrain, wid twelve women, no orficer's ladies, an' thirteen childer. We was to go six hundher' miles, an' railways was new in thim days. Whin we had been a night in the belly av the thrain —the men ragin' in their shirts an' dhrinkin' anything they cud find, an' eatin' bad fruit-stuff whin they cud, for we cudn't stop 'em—I was a Corp'ril thin—the cholera bruk out wid the dawnin' av the day.

"Pray to the Saints, you may niver see cholera in a throop-thrain! 'Tis like the judgmint av God hittin' down from the nakid sky! We run into a rest-camp—as ut might have been Ludianny, but not by any means so comfortable. The Orficer Commandin' sent a telegraft up the line, three hundher' mile up, askin' for help. Faith, we wanted ut, for ivry sowl av the followers ran for the dear life as soon as the thrain stopped; an' by the time that telegraft was writ, there wasn't a naygur in the station excepin' the telegraft-clerk—an' he only bekaze he was held down to his chair by the scruff av his sneakin' black neck. Thin the day began wid the noise in the carr'ges, an' the rattle av the men on the platform fillin' over, arms an' all, as they stud for to answer the Comp'ny muster-roll before goin' over to the camp. 'Tisn't for me to say what the cholera was like. Maybe the Doctor cud ha' tould, av he hadn't dropped on to the platform from the door av a carriage where he was takin' out the dead. He died wid the rest. Some bhoys had died in the night. We tuk out siven, and twenty more was sickenin' as we tuk thim. The women was huddled up any ways, screamin' wid fear.

"Sez the Commandin' Orficer whose name I mis-remember:—'Take the women over to that tope av trees yonder. Get thim out av the camp. 'Tis no place for thim.'

"Ould Pummeloe was sittin' on her beddin'-rowl, tryin' to kape little Jhansi quiet. 'Go off to that tope!' sez the Orficer. 'Go out av the men's way!'

" 'Be damned av I do!' sez Ould Pummeloe, an' little Jhansi, squattin' by her mother's side, squeaks out:—'Be damned av I do,' tu. Thin Ould Pummeloe turns to the women an' she sez:—'Are ye goin' to let the bhoys die while you're picnickin', ye sluts!' she sez. ' 'Tis wather they want. Come on an' help.'

"Wid that, she turns up her sleeves an' steps out for a well behind the rest-camp—little Jhansi trot-

tin' behind wid a *lotah* an' string, an' the other
women followin' like lambs, wid horse-buckets and
cookin' *degchies*. Whin all the things was full,
Ould Pummeloe marches back into camp—'twas
like a battlefield wid all the glory missin'—at the
hid av the rigimint av women.

" 'McKenna, me man!' she sez, wid a voice on
her like grand-roun's challenge, 'tell the bhoys to
be quiet. Ould Pummeloe's a-comin' to look afther
thim—wid free dhrinks.'

"Thin we cheered, and the cheerin' in the lines
was louder than the noise av the poor devils wid the
sickness on thim. But not much.

"You see, we was a new an' raw rigimint in those
days, an' we cud make neither head nor tail av the
sickness; an' so we was useless. The men was goin'
roun' an' about like dumb sheep, waitin' for the nex'
man to fall over, an' sayin' undher their spache:—
'Fwhat is ut? In the name av God, fwhat is ut?'
'Twas horrible. But through ut all, up an' down,
an' down an' up, wint Ould Pummeloe an' little
Jhansi—all we cud see av the baby, undher a dead
man's helmet wid the chin-strap swingin' about her
little stummick—up an' down wid the wather and
fwhat brandy there was.

"Now an' thin, Ould Pummeloe, the tears runnin' down her fat, red face, sez:—'Me bhoys, me
poor, dead darlin' bhoys!' But, for the most, she
was thryin' to put heart into the men an' kape thim
stiddy; and little Jhansi was tellin' thim all they

wud be "betther in the mornin'.' 'Twas a thrick she'd
picked up from hearing Ould Pummeloe whin Muttra was burnin' out wid fever. In the mornin'!
'Twas the iverlastin' mornin' at St. Peter's Gate
was the mornin' for seven an' twenty good men; an'
twenty more was sick to the death in that bitter,
burnin' sun. But the women worked like angils, as
I've said, an' the men like devils, till two doctors
come down from above, an' we was rescued.

"But, just before that, Ould Pummeloe, on her
knees over a bhoy in my squad—right-cot man to me
he was in the barrick—tellin' him the wurrud av
the Church that niver failed a man yet, sez:—
'Hould me up, bhoys! I'm feelin' bloody sick!'
'Twas the sun, not the cholera, did ut. She misremembered she was only wearin' her ould black
bonnet, an' she died wid 'McKenna, me man,' holdin'
her up, an' the bhoys howled whin they buried her.

"That night, a big wind blew, an' blew, an'
blew, an' blew the tents flat. But it blew the cholera
away an' niver another case there was all the while
we was waitin'—ten days in quarintin'. Av you will
belave me, the thrack of the sickness in the camp
was for all the worruld the thrack of a man walkin'
four times in a figure-av-eight through the tents.
They say 'tis the Wandherin' Jew takes the cholera
wid him. I believe it.

"An' that," said Mulvaney, illogically, "is the
cause why little Jhansi McKenna is fwhat she is.
She was brought up by the Quarter-Master Ser-

geant's wife whin McKenna died, but she b'longs to
B. Comp'ny; an' this tale I'm tellin' you—wid a
proper appreciashin av Jhansi McKenna—I've belted into every recruity av the Comp'ny as he was
drafted. Faith, 'twas me belted Corp'ril Slane into
askin' the girl!"

"Not really?"

"Man, I did! She's no beauty to look at, but
she's Ould Pummeloe's daughter, an' 'tis my juty to
provide for her. Just before Slane got his wan-
eight a day, I sez to him:—'Slane,' sez I, 'to-morrow
'twill be insubordinashin av me to chastise you; but,
by the sowl av Ould Pummeloe, who is now in glory,
av you don't give me your wurrud to ask Jhansi Mc-
Kenna at wanst, I'll peel the flesh off yer bones wid
a brass huk to-night. 'Tis a dishgrace to B. Com-
p'ny she's been single so long!' sez I. Was I goin'
to let a three-year-ould preshume to discoorse wid
me; my will bein' set? No! Slane wint and asked
her. He's a good bhoy is Slane. Wan av these
days he'll get into the Com'ssariat an' dhrive a boggy
wid his——savin's. So I provided for Ould Pummeloe's daughter; an' now you go along an' dance
wid her."

And I did.

I felt a respect for Miss Jhansi McKenna; and I
went to her wedding later on.

Perhaps I will tell you about that one of these
days.

THE MADNESS OF PRIVATE
ORTHERIS

THE MADNESS OF PRIVATE ORTHERIS

Oh! Where would I be when my froat was dry?
Oh! Where would I be when the bullets fly?
Oh! Where would I be when I come to die?
                    Why,
Somewheres anigh my chum.
    If 'e's liquor 'e'll give me some,
    If I'm dyin' 'e'll 'old my 'ead,
    An' 'e'll write 'em 'Ome when I'm dead.—
    Gawd send us a trusty chum!
                    Barrack Room Ballad.

My friends Mulvaney and Ortheris had gone on a shooting-expedition for one day. Learoyd was still in hospital, recovering from fever picked up in Burma. They sent me an invitation to join them, and were genuinely pained when I brought beer—almost enough beer to satisfy two Privates of the Line . . . . and Me.

"'Twasn't for that we bid you welkim, Sorr," said Mulvaney sulkily. "'Twas for the pleasure av your comp'ny."

Ortheris came to the rescue with:—"Well, 'e won't be none the worse for bringin' liquor with 'm. We ain't a file o' Dooks. We're bloomin' Tommies, ye cantankris Hirishman; an' 'ere's your very good 'ealth!"

We shot all the forenoon, and killed two pariah-dogs, four green parrots, sitting, one kite by the burning-ghaut, one snake flying, one mud-turtle, and eight crows. Game was plentiful. Then we sat down to tiffin—"bull-mate an' bran-bread," Mulvaney called it—by the side of the river, and took pot shots at the crocodiles in the intervals of cutting up the food with our only pocket-knife. Then we drank up all the beer, and threw the bottles into the water and fired at them. After that, we eased belts and stretched ourselves on the warm sand and smoked. We were too lazy to continue shooting.

Ortheris heaved a big sigh, as he lay on his stomach with his head between his fists. Then he swore quietly into the blue sky.

"Fwhat's that for?" said Mulvaney. "Have ye not drunk enough?"

"Tott'nim Court Road, an' a gal I fancied there. Wot's the good of sodgerin'?"

"Orth'ris, me son," said Mulvaney hastily, "'tis more than likely you've got throuble in your inside with the beer. I feel that way mesilf whin my liver gets rusty."

Ortheris went on slowly, not heeding the interruption:—

"I'm a Tommy—a bloomin', eight-anna, dog-stealin', Tommy, with a number instead of a decent name. Wot's the good o' me? If I 'ad a stayed at 'Ome, I might a' married that gal and a kep' a' little shorp in the 'Ammersmith 'Igh.—'S. Orth'ris, Prac-ti-cal Taxi-der-mist.' With a stuff' fox, like they 'as in the Halesbury Dairies, in the winder, an' a little case of blue and yaller glass-heyes, an' a little wife to call, 'shorp!' 'shorp!' when the door bell rung. As it his, I'm on'y a Tommy—a Bloomin', Gawd-forsaken, Beer-swillin', Tommy. 'Rest on your harms—'versed. Stan' at—hease; 'Shun. 'Verse—harms. Right an' lef'—tarrn. Slow—march. 'Alt—front. Rest on your harms—'versed. With blank-cartridge—load.' An' that's the end o' me."

He was quoting fragments from Funeral Parties' Orders.

"Stop ut!" shouted Mulvaney. "Whin you've fired into nothin' as often as me, over a better man than yoursilf, you will not make a mock av thim orders. 'Tis worse than whistlin' the Dead March in barricks. An' you full as a tick, an' the sun cool, an' all an' all! I take shame for you. You're no better than a Pagin—you an' your firin'-parties an' your glass-eyes. Won't you stop ut, Sorr?"

What could I do! Could I tell Ortheris anything that he did not know of the pleasures of his life? I was not a Chaplain nor a Subaltern, and Ortheris had a right to speak as he thought fit.

"Let him run, Mulvaney," I said. "It's the beer."

"No! 'Tisn't the beer," said Mulvaney. "I

know fwhat's comin'. He's tuk this way now an' agin, an' it's bad—it's bad—for I'm fond av the bhoy."

Indeed, Mulvaney seemed needlessly anxious; but I knew that he looked after Ortheris in a fatherly way.

"Let me talk, let me talk," said Ortheris, dreamily. "D'you stop your parrit screamin' of a 'ot day, when the cage is a-cookin' 'is pore little pink toes orf, Mulvaney?"

"Pink toes! D'ye mane to say you've pink toes under your bullswools, ye blandanderin',"—Mulvaney gathered himself together for a terrific denunciation—"school-mistress! Pink toes! How much Bass wid the label did that ravin' child dhrink?"

"'Tain't Bass," said Ortheris. "It's a bitterer beer nor that. It's 'ome-sickness!"

"Hark to him! An' he's goin Home in the *Sherapis* in the inside av four months!"

"I don't care. It's all one to me. 'Ow d'you know I ain't 'fraid o' dyin' 'fore I gets my papers?"

He recommenced, in a sing-song voice, the Funeral Orders.

I had never seen this side of Ortheris's character before, but evidently Mulvaney had, and attached serious importance to it. While Ortheris babbled, with his head on his arms, Mulvaney whispered to me:

"He's always tuk this way whin he's been checked

overmuch by the childher they make Sargints now-adays. That an' havin' nothin' to do. I can't make ut out anyways."

"Well, what does it matter? Let him talk himself through."

Ortheris began singing a parody of "The Ramrod Corps," full of cheerful allusions to battle, murder and sudden death. He looked out across the river as he sang; and his face was quite strange to me. Mulvaney caught me by the elbow to insure attention.

"Matther? It matther's everything! 'Tis some sort av fit that's on him. I've seen ut. 'Twill hould him all this night, an' in the middle av it, he'll get out av his cot and go rakin' in the rack for his 'couterments. Thin he'll come over to me an' say: —'I'm goin' to Bombay. Answer for me in the mornin'.' Thin me an' him will fight as we've done before—him to go an' me to hould him—an' so we'll both come on the books for disturbin' in barricks. I've belted him, an' I've bruk his head, an' I've talked to him, but 'tis no matter av use whin the fit's on him. He's as good a bhoy as ever stepped whin his mind's clear. I know fwhat's comin', though, this night in barricks. Lord send he doesn't losse off whin I rise for to knock him down. 'Tis that that's in my mind day an' night."

This put the case in a much less pleasant light, and fully accounted for Mulvaney's anxiety. He seemed to be trying to coax Ortheris out of the "fit"; for he shouted down the bank where the boy was lying:—

"Listen now, you wid the 'pore pink toes' an' the glass eyes! Did you shwim the Irriwaddy at night, behin' me, as a bhoy shud; or were you hidin' under a bed, as you was at Ahmed Kheyl?"

This was at once a gross insult and a direct lie, and Mulvaney meant it to bring on a fight. But Ortheris seemed shut up in some sort of trance. He answered slowly, without a sign of irritation, in the same cadenced voice as he had used for his firing-party orders:—

"Hi swum the Irriwaddy in the night, as you know, for to take the town of Lungtungpen, nakid an' without fear. Hand where I was at Ahmed Kheyl you know, and four bloomin' Pathans know, too. But that was summat to do, an' I didn't think o' dyin'. Now I'm sick to go 'Ome—go 'Ome—go 'Ome! No, I ain't mammy sick, because my uncle brung me up, but I'm sick for London again; sick for the sounds of 'er; an' the sights of 'er, and the stinks of 'er; orange-peel and hasphalte an' gas comin' in over Vaux'all Bridge. Sick for the rail goin' down into Box'Ill, with your gal on your knee an' a new clay pipe in your face. That, an' the Stran' lights where you knows ev'ryone, an' the Copper that takes you up is a old friend that tuk you up before, when you was a little, smitchy boy, lying loose 'tween the Temple an' the Dark Harches. No bloomin' guard-mountin', no bloomin' rottenstone, nor khaki, an' yourself your own master

with a gal to take an' see the Humaner's practisin'
ahookin' dead corpses out of the Serpentine o' Sundays. An' I lef' all that for to serve the Widder
beyond the seas where there ain't no women and
there ain't no liquor worth 'avin', and there ain't
nothin' to see, nor do, nor say, nor feel, nor think.
Lord love you, Stanley Orth'ris, but you're a bigger
bloomin' fool than the rest o' the reg'ment and
Mulvaney wired together! There's the Widder sittin' at 'Ome with a gold crown'd on 'er 'ead; and
'ere am Hi, Stanley Orth'ris, the Widder's property,
a rottin' FOOL!"

His voice rose at the end of the sentence, and he
wound up with a six-shot Anglo-Vernacular oath.
Mulvaney said nothing, but looked at me as if he
expected that I could bring peace to poor Ortheris's
troubled brain.

I remembered once at Rawal Pindi having seen
a man, nearly mad with drink, sobered by being
made a fool of. Some regiments may know what
I mean. I hoped that we might shake off Ortheris
in the same way, though he was perfectly sober:
So I said:—

"What's the use of grousing there, and speaking
against The Widow?"

"I didn't!" said Ortheris. "S'elp me Gawd, I
never said a word agin 'er, an' I wouldn't—not if
I was to desert this minute!"

Here was my opening. "Well, you meant to,
anyhow. What's the use of cracking on for noth-

ing? Would you slip it now if you got the chance?"

"On'y try me!" said Ortheris, jumping to his feet as if he had been stung.

Mulvaney jumped too. "Fwhat are you going to do?" said he.

"Help Ortheris down to Bombay or Karachi, whichever he likes. You can report that he separated from you before tiffin, and left his gun on the bank here!"

"I'm to report that—am I?" said Mulvaney, slowly. "Very well. If Orth'ris manes to desert now, and will desert now, an' you, Sorr, who have been a friend to me an' to him, will help him to ut, I, Terrence Mulvaney, on my oath which I've never bruk yet, will report as you say. But"—here he stepped up to Ortheris, and shook the stock of the fowling-piece in his face—"your fistes help you, Stanley Orth'ris, if ever I come across you agin!"

"I don't care!" said Ortheris. "I'm sick o' this dorg's life. Give me a chanst. Don't play with me. Le' me go!"

"Strip," said I, "and change with me, and then I'll tell you what to do."

I hoped that the absurdity of this would check Ortheris; but he had kicked off his ammunition-boots and got rid of his tunic almost before I had loosed my shirt-collar. Mulvaney gripped me by the arm:—

"The fit's on him: the fit's workin' on him still. By my Honor and Sowl, we shall be accessiry to a desartion yet; only twenty-eight days, as you say, Sorr, or fifty-six, but think o' the shame—the black shame to him an' me!" I had never seen Mulvaney so excited.

But Ortheris was quite calm, and, as soon as he had exchanged clothes with me, and I stood up a Private of the Line, he said shortly:—

"Now! Come on. What nex'? D'ye mean fair. What must I do to get out o' this 'ere a Hell?"

I told him that, if he would wait for two or three hours near the river, I would ride into the Station and come back with one hundred rupees. He would, with that money in his pocket, walk to the nearest side-station on the line, about five miles away, and would there take a first-class ticket for Karachi. Knowing that he had no money on him when he went out shooting, his regiment would not immediately wire to the seaports, but would hunt for him in the native villages near the river. Further, no one would think of seeking a deserter in a first-class carriage. At Karachi, he was to buy white clothes and ship, if he could, on a cargo-steamer.

Here he broke in. If I helped him to Karachi, he would arrange all the rest. Then I ordered him to wait where he was until it was dark enough for me to ride into the station without my dress being noticed. Now God in His wisdom has made the heart of the British Soldier, who is very often an unlicked ruffian, as soft as the heart of a little child, in order that he may believe in and follow his officers into tight and nasty places. He does not so readily come to believe in a "civilian" but, when he does, he believes implicitly and like a dog. I had had the honor of the friendship of Private Ortheris, at intervals, for more than three years, and we had dealt with each other as man by man. Consequently, he considered that all my words were true, and not spoken lightly.

Mulvaney and I left him in the high grass near the river-bank, and went away, still keeping to the high grass, towards my horse. The shirt scratched me horribly.

We waited nearly two hours for the dusk to fall and allow me to ride off. We spoke of Ortheris in whispers, and strained our ears to catch any sound from the spot where we had left him. But we heard nothing except the wind in the plume-grass.

"I've bruk his head," said Mulvaney, earnestly, "time an' agin. I've nearly kilt him wid the belt, an' yet I can't knock thim fits out ov his soft head. No! An' he's not soft, for he's reason-able an' likely by natur'. Fwhat is ut? Is ut his breedin' which is nothin', or his edukashin which he niver got? You that think ye know things, answer me that."

But I found no answer. I was wondering how long Ortheris, in the bank of the river, would hold out, and whether I should be forced to help him to desert, as I had given my word.

Just as the dusk shut down and, with a very heavy heart, I was beginning to saddle up my horse, we heard wild shouts from the river.

The devils had departed from Private Stanley Ortheris, No. 22639, B. Company. The loneliness, the dusk, and the waiting had driven them out as I had hoped. We set off at the double and found him plunging about wildly through the grass, with his coat off—my coat off, I mean. He was calling for us like a madman.

When we reached him, he was dripping with perspiration, and trembling like a startled horse. We had great difficulty in soothing him. He complained that he was in a civilian kit, and wanted to tear my clothes off his body. I ordered him to strip, and we made a second exchange as quickly as possible.

The rasp of his own "grayback" shirt and the squeak of his boots seemed to bring him to himself. He put his hands before his eyes and said:—

"Wot was it? I ain't mad, I ain't sunstrook, an' I've bin an' gone an' said, an' bin an' gone an' done. . . . . Wot 'ave I bin an' done!"

"Fwhat have you done?" said Mulvaney. "You've dishgraced yourself—though that's no worst av all, you've dishgraced Me! Me that taught you how for to walk abroad like a man —when you was a dhirty little, fish-backed little, whimperin' little recruity. As you are now, Stanley Orth'ris!"

Ortheris said nothing for awhile. Then he unslung his belt, heavy with the badges of half-a-dozen regiments that his own had lain with, and handed it over to Mulvaney.

"I'm too little for to mill you, Mulvaney," said he, "an' you've strook me before; but you can take an' cut me in two with this 'ere if you like."

Mulvaney turned to me.

"Lave me talk to him, Sorr," said Mulvaney.

I left, and on my way home thought a good deal over Ortheris in particular, and my friend, Private Thomas Atkins, whom I love, in general.

But I could not come to any conclusion of any kind whatever.

THE BISARA OF POOREE

THE BISARA OF POOREE

Little Blind Fish, thou art marvelous wise,
Little Blind Fish, who put out thy eyes?
Open thine ears while I whisper my wish—
Bring me a lover, thou little Blind Fish.
The Charm of the Bisara.

SOME natives say that it came from the other side
of Kulu, where the eleven-inch Temple Sapphire
is. Others that it was made at the Devil-Shrine
of Ao-Chung in Thibet, was stolen by a Kafir,
from him by a Gurkha, from him again by a La-
houli, from him by a *khitmatgar*, and by this latter sold to an Englishman, so all its virtue was
lost: because, to work properly, the Bisara of Pooree
must be stolen—with bloodshed if possible, but, at
any rate, stolen.

These stories of the coming into India are all
false. It was made at Pooree ages since—the
manner of its making would fill a small book—
was stolen by one of the Temple dancing-girls
there, for her own purposes, and then passed on
from hand to hand, steadily northward, till it
reached Hanlá: always bearing the same name—
the Bisara of Pooree. In shape it is a tiny, square
box of silver, studded outside with eight small

balas-rubies. Inside the box, which opens with a
spring, is a little, eyeless fish, carved from some
sort of dark, shiny nut and wrapped in a shred
of faded gold-cloth. That is the Bisara of Pooree,
and it were better for a man to take a king
cobra in his hand than to touch the Bisara of
Pooree.

All kinds of magic are out of date, and done
away with except in India where nothing changes
in spite of the shiny, top-scum stuff that people
call "civilization." Any man who knows about
the Bisara of Pooree will tell you what its powers
are—always supposing that it has been honestly
stolen. It is the only regularly working, trust-
worthy love-charm in the country, with one ex-
ception.

[The other charm is in the hands of a trooper
of the Nizam's Horse, at a place called Tuprani,
due north of Hyderabad.] This can be de-
pended upon for a fact. Some one else may explain it.

If the Bisara be not stolen, but given or bought
or found, it turns against its owner in three years,
and leads to ruin or death. This is another fact
which you may explain when you have time. Mean-
while, you can laugh at it. At present, the Bisara
is safe on an *ekka*-pony's neck, inside the blue
bead-necklace that keeps off the Evil-eye. If the
ekka-driver ever finds it, and wears it, or gives it
to his wife, I am sorry for him.

A very dirty hill-cooly woman, with goitre, owned it at Theog in 1884. It came into Simla from the north before Churton's *khitmatgar* bought it, and sold it, for three times its silver-value, to Churton, who collected curiosities. The servant knew no more what he had bought than the master; but a man looking over Churton's collection of curiosities—Churton was an Assistant Commissioner by the way—saw and held his tongue. He was an Englishman; but knew how to believe. Which shows that he was different from most Englishmen. He knew that it was dangerous to have any share in the little box when working or dormant; for unsought Love is a terrible gift.

Pack—"Grubby" Pack, as we used to call him—was, in every way, a nasty little man who must have crawled into the Army by mistake. He was three inches taller than his sword, but not half so strong. And the sword was a fifty-shilling, tailor-made one. Nobody liked him, and, I suppose, it was his wizenedness and worthlessness that made him fall so hopelessly in love with Miss Hollis, who was good and sweet, and five foot seven in her tennis-shoes. He was not content with falling in love quietly, but brought all the strength of his miserable little nature into the business. If he had not been so objectionable, one might have pitied him. He vapored, and fretted, and fumed, and trotted up and down, and tried to make himself pleasing in Miss Hollis's big, quiet, gray eyes, and failed. It was one of the cases that you sometimes meet, even in this country where we marry by Code, of a really blind attachment all on one side, without the faintest possibility of return. Miss Hollis looked on Pack as some sort of vermin running about the road. He had no prospects beyond Captain's pay, and no wits to help that out by one anna. In a large-sized man, love like this would have been touching. In a good man it would have been grand. He being what he was, it was only a nuisance.

You will believe this much. What you will not believe, is what follows: Churton, and The Man who Knew what the Bisara was, were lunching at the Simla Club together. Churton was complaining of life in general. His best mare had rolled out of the stable down the hill and had broken her back; his decisions were being reversed by the upper Courts more than an Assistant Commissioner of eight years' standing has a right to expect; he knew liver and fever, and, for weeks past, had felt out of sorts. Altogether, he was disgusted and disheartened.

Simla Club dining-room is built, as all the world knows, in two sections, with an arch-arrangement dividing them. Come in, turn to your own left, take the table under the window, and you cannot see any one who has come in, turned to the right, and taken a table on the right side of the arch. Curiously enough, every word that you say can be heard, not only by the other diner, but by the servants beyond the screen through which they bring dinner. This is worth knowing: an echoing-room is a trap to be forewarned against.

Half in fun, and half hoping to be believed, The Man who Knew told Churton the story of the Bisara of Pooree at rather greater length than I have told it to you in this place; winding up with a suggestion that Churton might as well throw the little box down hill and see whether all his troubles would go with it. In ordinary ears, English ears, the tale was only an interesting bit of folk-lore. Churton laughed, said that he felt better for his tiffin, and went out. Pack had been tiffining by himself to the right of the arch, and had heard everything. He was nearly mad with his absurd infatuation for Miss Hollis, that all Simla had been laughing about.

It is a curious thing that, when a man hates or loves beyond reason, he is ready to go beyond reason to gratify his feelings. Which he would not do for money or power merely. Depend upon it, Solomon would never have built altars to Ashtorath and all those ladies with queer names, if there had not been trouble of some kind in his *zennana*, and nowhere else. But this is beside the story. The facts of the case are these: Pack called on Churton next day when Churton was out, left his card, and stole the Bisara of Pooree from its place under the clock on the mantel-piece! Stole it like the thief he was by nature. Three days later, all Simla was electrified by the news that Miss Hollis had accepted Pack—the shriveled rat, Pack! Do you desire clearer evidence than this? The Bisara of Pooree had been stolen, and it worked as it had always done when won by foul means.

There are three or four times in a man's life when he is justified in meddling with other people's affairs to play Providence.

The Man who Knew felt that he was justified; but believing and acting on a belief are quite different things. The insolent satisfaction of Pack as he ambled by the side of Miss Hollis, and Churton's striking release from liver, as soon as the Bisara of Pooree had gone, decided the Man. He explained to Churton, and Churton laughed, because he was not brought up to believe that men on the Government House List steal—at least little things. But the miraculous acceptance by Miss Hollis of that tailor, Pack, decided him to take steps on suspicion. He vowed that he only wanted to find out where his ruby-studded silver box had vanished to. You cannot accuse a man on the Government House List of stealing. And if you rifle his room, you are a thief yourself. Churton, prompted by The Man who Knew, decided on burglary. If he found nothing in Pack's room . . . . but it is not nice to think of what would have happened in that case.

Pack went to a dance at Benmore—Benmore was Benmore in those days, and not an office— and danced fifteen waltzes out of twenty-two with Miss Hollis. Churton and The Man took all the keys that they could lay hands on, and went to Pack's room in the hotel, certain that his servants would be away. Pack was a cheap soul. He had not purchased a decent cash-box to keep his papers in, but one of those native imitations that you buy for ten rupees. It opened to any sort of key, and there at the bottom, under Pack's Insurance Policy, lay the Bisara of Pooree!

Churton called Pack names, put the Bisara of Pooree in his pocket, and went to the dance with The Man. At least, he came in time for supper, and saw the beginning of the end in Miss Hollis's eyes. She was hysterical after supper, and was taken away by her Mama.

At the dance with the abominable Bisara in his pocket, Churton twisted his foot on one of the steps leading down to the old Rink, and had to be sent home in a 'rickshaw, grumbling. He did not believe in the Bisara of Pooree any the more for this manifestation, but he sought out Pack and called him some ugly names; and "thief" was the mildest of them. Pack took the names with the nervous smile of a little man who wants both soul and body to resent an insult, and went his way. There was no public scandal.

A week later, Pack got his definite dismissal from Miss Hollis. There had been a mistake in the placing of her affection, she said. So he went away to Madras, where he can do no great harm even if he lives to be a Colonel.

Churton insisted upon The Man who Knew taking the Bisara of Pooree as a gift. The Man took it, went down to the Cart-Road at once, found an *ekka*-pony with a blue bead-necklace, fastened the Bisara of Pooree inside the necklace with a piece of shoe-string and thanked Heaven that he was rid of a danger. Remember, in case you ever find it, that you must not destroy the Bisara of Pooree. I have not time to explain why just now, but the power lies in the little wooden fish. Mister Gubernatis or Max Müller could tell you more about it than I.

You will say that all this story is made up, Very well. If ever you come across a little, silver, ruby-studded box, seven-eighths of an inch long by three-quarters wide, with a dark-brown wooden fish, wrapped in gold cloth, inside it, keep it. Keep it for three years, and then you will discover for yourself whether my story is true or false.

Better still, steal it as Pack did, and you will be sorry that you had not killed yourself in the beginning.

A CONFERENCE OF THE
POWERS

A CONFERENCE OF THE POWERS

"Life liveth best in life, and doth not roam
To other realms if all be well at home,
'Solid as ocean foam,' quoth ocean foam."

THE room was blue with the smoke of three pipes
and a cigar. The leave season had opened in India,
and the first-fruits on the English side of the water
were "Tick" Boileau, of the Forty-fifth Bengal
Cavalry, who called on me after three years' ab-
sence to discuss old things which had happened.
Fate, who always does her work handsomely, sent
up the same staircase within the same hour the
Infant, fresh from Upper Burmah, and he and
Boileau, looking out of my window, saw walking
in the street one Nevin, late in a Ghoorkha regiment and the Black Mountain expedition. They
yelled to him to come up, and the whole street
was aware that they desired him to come up; and
he came up, and there followed pandemonium, because we had foregathered from the ends of the
earth, and three of us were on a holiday, and none
of us was twenty-five, and all the delights of all
London lay waiting our pleasure.

Boileau took the only other chair; and the Infant, by right of his bulk, the sofa; and Nevin,

being a little man, sat cross-legged on the top of the revolving bookcase; and we all said: "who'd ha' thought it?" and "what are you doing here?" till speculation was exhausted, and the talk went over to inevitable "shop". Boileau was full of a great scheme for securing military attachéship at St. Petersburg; Nevin had hopes of the Staff College; and the Infant had been moving heaven and earth and the Horse Guards for a commission in the Egyptian army.

"What's the use o' that?" said Nevin twirling round on the bookcase.

"Oh, heaps! Course if you get stuck with a Fellaheen regiment, you're sold; but if you are appointed to a Soudanese lot, you're in clover. They are first-class fighting men, and just think of the eligible, central position of Egypt in the next row!"

This was putting the match to a magazine. We all began to explain the Central-Asian question off-hand, flinging army corps from the Helmund to Cashmir with more than Russian recklessness. Each of the boys made for himself a war to his own liking, and when we had settled all the details of Armageddon, killed all our senior officers, handled a division apiece, and nearly torn the atlas in two in attempts to explain our theories, Boileau needs must lift up his voice above the clamor and cry: "Anyhow, it'll be the——of a row!" in tones that carried conviction far down the staircase.

Entered unperceived in the smoke William the Silent. "Gen'leman to see you, sir," said he, and disappeared, leaving in his stead none other than Mr. Eustace Cleever. William would have introduced the dragon of Wantley with equal disregard of present company.

"I—I beg your pardon! I didn't know that there was anybody—with you. I—"

But it was not seemly to allow Mr. Cleever to depart, for he was a great man. The boys remained where they were, because any movement would block the little room. Only when they saw his gray hairs they stood up on their feet, and when the Infant caught the name, he said: "Are you—did you write that book called 'As it was in the Beginning'?"

Mr. Cleever admitted that he had written the book.

"Then—then I don't know how to thank you, sir," said the Infant, flushing pink. "I was brought up in the country you wrote about. All my people live there, and I read the book in camp out in Burmah on the Hlinedatalone, and I knew every stick and stone, and the dialect, too; and, by Jove! it was just like being at home and hearing the country people talk. Nevin, you know 'As it was in the Beginning'? So does Ti— Boileau."

Mr. Cleever has tasted as much praise, public and private, as one man may safely swallow, but it seemed to me that the outspoken admiration in the Infant's eyes and the little stir in the little company came home to him very nearly indeed.

"Won't you take the sofa?" said the Infant. "I'll sit on Boileau's chair, and—" Here he looked at me to spur me to my duties as a host, but I was watching the novelist's face.   Cleever had not the least intention of going away, but settled himself on the sofa.   Following the first great law of the army, which says: "All property is common except money, and you've only got to ask the next man for that," the Infant offered tobacco and drink.   It was the least he could do, but not four columns of the finest review in the world held half as much appreciation and reverence as the Infant's simple: "Say when, sir," above the long glass.

Cleever said "when," and more thereto, for he was a golden talker, and he sat in the midst of hero-worship devoid of all taint of self-interest. The boys asked him of the birth of his book, and whether it was hard to write, and how his notions came to him, and he answered with the same absolute simplicity, as he was questioned.   His big eyes twinkled, he dug his long, thin hands into his gray beard, and tugged it as he grew animated and dropped little by little from the peculiar pinching of the broader vowels—the indefinable "euh"

that runs through the speech of the pundit caste
—and the elaborate choice of words to freely
mouthed ows and ois, and for him, at least, unfet-
tered colloquialisms. He could not altogether
understand the boys who hung upon his words so
reverently. The line of the chin-strap that still
showed white and untanned on cheek-bone and
jaw, the steadfast young eyes puckered at the
corners of the lids with much staring through
red-hot sunshine, the deep, troubled breathing,
and the curious crisp, curt speech seemed to
puzzle him equally. He could create men and women, and send them to the uttermost ends of the
earth to help, delight, and comfort; he knew every
mood of the fields, and could interpret them to the
cities, and he knew the hearts of many in the
city and country, but he had hardly in forty years
come into contact with the thing which is called
A Subaltern of the Line. He told the boys
this.

"Well, how should you?" said the Infant. "You
—you're quite different, y' see, sir."

The Infant expressed his ideas in his tone rather
than his words, and Cleever understood the compliments.

"We're only subs," said Nevin, "and we aren't
exactly the sort of men you'd meet much in your
life, I s'pose."

"That's true," said Cleever. "I live chiefly
among those who write and paint and sculp and

so forth. We have our own talk and our own interests, and the outer world doesn't trouble us much."

"That must be awf'ly jolly," said Boileau, at a venture. "We have our own shop too, but 'tisn't half as interesting as yours, of course. You know all the men who've ever done anything, and we only knock about from place to place, and we do nothing."

"The army's a very lazy profession, if you choose to make it so," said Nevin. "When there's nothing going on, there is nothing going on, and you lie up."

"Or try to get a billet somewhere so as to be ready for the next show," said the Infant, with a chuckle.

"To me," said Cleever, softly, "the whole idea of warfare seems so foreign and unnatural—so essentially vulgar, if I may say so—that I can hardly appreciate your sensations. Of course, though, any change from idling in garrison towns must be a godsend to you."

Like not a few home-staying Englishmen, Cleever believed that the newspaper phrase he quoted covered the whole duty of the army, whose toil enabled him to enjoy his many-sided life in peace. The remark was not a happy one, for Boileau had just come off the Indian frontier, the Infant had been on the war-path for nearly eighteen months, and the little red man, Nevin, two months before had been sleeping under the stars at the peril of his life. But none of them tried to explain till I ventured to point out that they had all seen service, and were not used to idling. Cleever took in the idea slowly.

"Seen service?" said he. Then, as a child might ask, "Tell me—tell me everything about everything."

"How do you mean, sir?" said the Infant, delighted at being directly appealed to by the great man.

"Good heavens! how am I to make you understand if you can't see? In the first place, what is your age?"

"Twenty-three next July," said the Infant, promptly.

Cleever questioned the others with his eyes.

"I'm twenty-four," said Nevin.

"I'm twenty-two," said Boileau.

"And you've all seen service?"

"We've all knocked about a little bit, sir, but the Infant's the war-worn veteran. He's had two years' work in Upper Burmah," said Nevin.

"When you say work, what do you mean, you extraordinary creatures?"

"Explain it, Infant," said Nevin.

"Oh, keeping things in order generally, and running about after little *dakus*—that's Dacoits—and so on. There's nothing to explain."

"Make that young leviathan speak," said Cleever, impatiently.

"How can he speak?" said I. "He's done the work. The two don't go together. But, Infant, you are requested to *bukh*."

"What about? I'll try."

"*Bukh* about a *daur*. You've been on heaps of 'em," said Nevin.

"What in the world does that mean? Has the army a language of its own?"

The Infant turned very red. He was afraid he was being laughed at, and he detested talking before outsiders; but it was the author of "As it was in the Beginning" who waited.

"It's all so new to me," pleaded Cleever. "And —and you said you liked my book."

This was a direct appeal that the Infant could understand. He began, rather flurriedly, with "Pull me up, sir, if I say anything you don't follow. 'Bout six months before I took my leave out of Burmah I was on the Hlinedatalone up near the Shan states with sixty Tommies—private soldiers, that is—and another subaltern, a year senior to me. The Burmese business was a subaltern war, and our forces were split up into little detachments, all running about the country and trying to keep the Dacoits quiet. The Dacoits were having a first-class time, y' know—filling women up with kerosene and setting 'em alight, and burning villages, and crucifying people."

The wonder in Eustace Cleever's eyes deepened. He disbelieved wholly in a book which describes crucifixion at length, and he could not quite realize that the custom still existed.

"Have you ever seen a crucifixion?" said he.

"Of course not. Shouldn't have allowed it if I had. But I've seen the corpses. The Dacoits had a nice trick of sending a crucified corpse down the river on a raft, just to show they were keeping their tail up and enjoying themselves. Well, that was the kind of people I had to deal with."

"Alone?" said Cleever. Solitude of the soul he knew—none better; but he had never been ten miles away from his fellow-men in his life.

"I had my men, but the rest of it was pretty much alone. The nearest military post that could give me orders was fifteen miles away, and we used to heliograph to them, and they used to give us orders the same way. Too many orders."

"Who was your C. O.?" said Boileau.

"Bounderby. Major. *Pukka* Bounderby. More Bounder than *pukka*. He went out up Bhamo way. Shot or cut down last year," said the Infant.

"What mean these interludes in a strange tongue?" said Cleever to me.

"Professional information, like the Mississippi pilots' talk. He did not approve of his major, who has since died a violent death," said I. "Go on, Infant."

"Far too many orders. You couldn't take the Tommies out for a two-days' daur—that means expedition, sir—without being blown up for not asking leave. And the whole country was humming with Dacoits. I used to send out spies and act on their information. As soon as a man came in and told me of a gang in hiding, I'd take thirty men, with some grub, and go out and look for them, while the other subaltern lay doggo in camp."

"Lay? Pardon me, but how did he lie?" said Cleever.

"Lay doggo. Lay quiet with the other thirty men. When I came back, he'd take out his half of the command, and have a good time of his own."

"Who was he?" said Boileau.

"Carter-Deecy, of the Aurangabadis. Good chap, but too *zubberdusty* and went *bokhar* four days out of seven. He's gone out too. Don't interrupt a man."

Cleever looked helplessly at me.

"The other subaltern," I translate, swiftly, "came from a native regiment and was overbearing in his demeanor. He suffered much from the fever of the country, and is now dead. Go on, Infant."

"After a bit we got into trouble for using the men on frivolous occasions, and so I used to put my signaler under arrest to prevent him reading the helio orders. Then I'd go out and leave a message to be sent an hour after I got clear of the camp; something like this: 'Received important information; start in an hour, unless countermanded.' If I was ordered back, it didn't much matter. I swore that the C. O.'s watch was wrong, or something, when I came back. The Tommies enjoyed the fun, and—oh, yes—there was one Tommy who was the bard of the detachment. He used to make up verses on everything that happened."

"What sort of verses?" said Cleever.

"Lovely verses; and the Tommies used to sing 'em. There was one song with a chorus, and it said something like this." The Infant dropped into the barrack-room twang:

" 'Theebau, the Burmah king, did a very foolish thing
    When 'e mustered 'ostile forces in ar-rai.
'E littul thought that we, from far across the sea,
    Would send our armies up to Mandalai!' "

"Oh, gorgeous!" said Cleever. "And how magnificently direct! The notion of a regimental bard is new to me. It's epic."

"He was awf'ly popular with the men," said the Infant. "He had them all down in rhyme as soon as ever they had done anything. He was a great bard. He was always on time with a eulogy when we picked up a Boh—that's a leader of Dacoits."

"How did you pick him up?" said Cleever.

"Oh, shot him if he wouldn't surrender."

"You! Have you shot a man?"

There was a subdued chuckle from all three, and it dawned on the questioner that one experience in life which was denied to himself—and he weighed the souls of men in a balance—had been shared by three very young gentlemen of engaging appearance. He turned round on Nevin, who had climbed to the top of the bookcase and was sitting cross-legged as before.

"And have you, too?"

"Think so," said Nevin, sweetly. "In the Black Mountain, sir. He was rolling cliffs on to my half-company and spoiling our formation. I took a rifle from a man and brought him down at the second shot."

"Good heavens! And how did you feel afterward?"

"Thirsty. I wanted a smoke, too."

Cleever looked at Boileau, the youngest. Surely his hands were guiltless of blood. Boileau shook his head and laughed. "Go on, Infant," said he.

"And you, too?" said Cleever.

"Fancy so. It was a case of cut—cut or be cut—with me, so I cut at one. I couldn't do any more, sir," said Boileau.

Cleever looked as though he would like to ask many questions, but the Infant swept on in the full tide of his tale.

"Well, we were called insubordinate young whelps at last, and strictly forbidden to take the Tommies out any more without orders. I wasn't sorry, because Tommy is such an exacting sort of creature, though he works beautifully. He wants to live as though he were in barracks all the time. I was grubbing on fowls and boiled corn, but the Tommies wanted their pound of fresh meat, and their half ounce of this, and their two ounces of t'other thing, and they used to come to me and badger me for plug tobacco when we were four days in jungle! I said: 'I can get you Burmah tobacco, but I don't keep a canteen up my sleeve.' They couldn't see it. They wanted all the luxuries of the season, confound 'em!"

"You were alone when you were dealing with these men?" said Cleever, watching the Infant's face under the palm of his hand. He was receiving new ideas, and they seemed to trouble him.

"Of course. Unless you count the mosquitoes. They were nearly as big as the men. After I had to lie doggo I began to look for something to do, and I was great pals with a man called Hicksey, in the Burmah police—the best man that ever stepped on earth; a first-class man."

Cleever nodded applause. He knew something of enthusiasm.

"Hicksey and I were as thick as thieves. He had some Burmah mounted police—nippy little

chaps, armed with sword and Snider carbine.
They rode punchy Burmah ponies, with string
stirrups, red cloth saddles, and red bell-rope head-
stalls. Hicksey used to lend me six or eight of
them when I asked him—nippy little devils, keen
as mustard. But they told their wives too much,
and all my plans got known, till I learned to give
false marching orders overnight, and take the
men to quite a different village in the morning.
Then we used to catch the simple *dakus* before
breakfast, and make them very sick. It's a
ghastly country on the Hlinedatalone; all bamboo
jungle, with paths about four feet wide winding
through it. The *dakus* knew all the paths, and
used to pot at us as we came round a corner;
but the mounted police knew the paths as well as
the *dakus*, and we used to go stalking 'em in and
out among the paths. Once we flushed 'em—the
men on the ponies had the pull of the man on
foot. We held all the country absolutely quiet for
ten miles round in about a month. Then we took
Boh Naghee—Hicksey and I and the civil officer.
That was a lark!"

"I think I am beginning to understand a little,"
said Cleever. "It was a pleasure to you to ad-
minister and fight, and so on."

"Rather. There's nothing nicer than a satisfactory little expedition, when you find all your
plans fit together and your conformations *teek*
—correct, you know—and the whole *subchiz*—

I mean when everything works out like formulæ on a blackboard. Hicksey had all the information about the Boh. He had been burning villages and murdering pepole right and left, and cutting up government convoys, and all that. He was lying doggo in a village about fifteen miles off, waiting to get a fresh gang together. So we arranged to take thirty mounted police, and turn him out before he could plunder into the newly settled villages. At the last minute the civil officer in our part of the world thought he'd assist in the performance."

"Who was he?" said Nevin.

"His name was Dennis," said the Infant, slowly; "and we'll let it stay so. He's a better man now than he was then."

"But how old was the civil power?" said Cleever. "The situation is developing itself." Then, in his beard: "Who are you, to judge men?"

"He was about six-and-twenty," said the Infant; "and he was awf'ly clever. He knew a lot of literary things, but I don't think he was quite steady enough for Dacoit-hunting. We started overnight for Boh Na-ghee's villages, and we got there just before the morning, without raising an alarm. Dennis had turned out armed to the teeth—two revolvers, a carbine, and all sorts of things. I was talking to Hicksey about posting our men, and Dennis edged his pony in between us, and said: 'What shall I do? What shall I do? Tell me what to do, you fellows.' We didn't take much notice, but his pony tried to bite me in the leg, and I said: 'Pull out a bit, old mán, till we've settled the attack.' He kept edging in, and fiddling with his reins and the revolvers, and saying: 'Dear me! dear me! Oh dear me! What do you think I'd better do?' The man was in a blue funk and his teeth were chattering."

"I sympathize with the civil power," said Cleever. "Continue, young Clive."

"The fun of it was that he was supposed to be our superior officer. Hicksey took a good look at him, and told him to attach himself to my party. Beastly mean of Hicksey, that. The chap kept on edging in and bothering, instead of asking for some men and taking up his own position, till I got angry. The carbines began popping on the other side of the village. Then I said: 'For God's sake, be quiet, and sit down where you are! If you see anybody come out of the village, shoot at him.' I knew he couldn't hit a hayrick at a yard. Then I took my men over the garden wall —over the palisades, y' know—somehow or other, and the fun began. Hicksey had found the Boh in bed under a mosquito curtain, and he had taken a flying jump on to him."

"A flying jump?" said Cleever. "Is that also war?"

"Yes," said the Infant, now thoroughly warmed. "Don't you know how you take a flying

jump on to a fellow's head at school when he
snores in the dormitory? The Boh was sleeping
in a regular bedful of swords and pistols, and
Hicksey came down *a la* Zazel through the netting,
and the net got mixed up with the pistols and
the Boh and Hicksey, and they all rolled on the
floor together. I laughed till I couldn't stand,
and Hicksey was cursing me for not helping him,
so I left him to fight it out, and went into the
village. Our men were slashing about and firing,
and so were the Dacoits, and in the thick of the
mess some ass set fire to a house, and we all had
to clear out. I froze on to the nearest *daku*,
and ran to the palisade, shoving him in front of
me. He wriggled clear and bounded over to the
other side. I came after him, but when I had
one leg one side and one leg the other of the
palisade, I saw that my friend had fallen flat
on Dennis's head. That man had never moved
from where I left him. The two rolled on the
ground together, and Dennis's carbine went off
and nearly shot me. The *daku* picked himself
up and ran, and Dennis heaved his carbine after
him, and it caught him on the back of his head
and knocked him silly. You never saw anything
so funny in your life. I doubled up on the top
of the palisade and hung there, yelling with
laughter. But Dennis began to weep like anything. 'Oh, I've killed a man!' he said—'I've
killed a man, and I shall never know another

peaceful hour in my life! Is he dead? Oh, is he dead? Good God! I've killed a man!' I came down and said: 'Don't be a fool!' But he kept on shouting 'Is he dead?' till I could have kicked him. The *daku* was only knocked out of time with the carbine. He came to after a bit, and I said: 'Are you hurt much?' He grinned and said no. His chest was all cut with scrambling over the palisade. 'The white man's gun didn't do that,' he said. 'I did that myself, and I knocked the white man over.' Just like a Burman, wasn't it? Dennis wouldn't be happy at any price. He said: 'Tie up his wounds. He'll bleed to death. Oh, my God, he'll bleed to death!' 'Tie 'em up yourself,' I said, 'if you're so anxious.' 'I can't touch him,' said Dennis, 'but here's my shirt.' He took off his shirt, and he fixed his braces again over his bare shoulders. I ripped the shirt up and bandaged the Dacoit quite professionally. He was grinning at Dennis all the time; and Dennis's haversack was lying on the ground, bursting full of sandwiches. Greedy hog! I took some and offered some to Dennis. 'How can I eat?' he said. 'How can you ask me to eat? His very blood is on your hands, oh, God! and you're eating my sandwiches!' 'All right,' I said. 'I'll give 'em to the *daku*.' So I did, and the little chap was quite pleased, and wolfed 'em down like one o'clock.''

Cleever brought his hand down on the tablecloth a thump that made the empty glasses dance. "That's art," he said. "Flat, flagrant mechanism. Don't tell me that happened on the spot!"

The pupils of the Infant's eyes contracted to pin points. "I beg your pardon," he said slowly and a little stiffly, "but I am telling this thing as it happened."

Cleever looked at him for a moment. "My fault entirely," said he. "I should have known. Please go on."

"Oh, then Hicksey came out of what was left of the village with his prisoners and captives all neatly tied up. Boh Na-ghee was first, and one of the villagers, as soon as he saw the old ruffian helpless, began kicking him quietly. The Boh stood it as long as he could, and then groaned, and we saw what was going on. Hicksey tied the villager up and gave him half a dozen good ones to remind him to leave a prisoner alone. You should have seen the old Boh grin. Oh, but Hicksey was in a furious rage with everybody. He'd got a wipe over the elbow that had tickled up his funny-bone, and he was simply rabid with me for not having helped him with the Boh and the mosquito net. I had to explain that I couldn't do anything. If you'd seen 'em both tangled up together on the floor, like a blaspheming cocoon, you'd have laughed for a week. Hicksey swore that the only decent man of his acquaintance was the Boh, and all the way back to camp Hicksey was talking to him, and the Boh was grumbling about the soreness of his bones. When we got home and had had a bath, the Boh wanted to know when he was going to be hanged. Hicksey said he couldn't oblige him on the spot, but had to send him to Rangoon. The Boh went down on his knees and reeled off a catalogue of his crimes —he ought to have been hanged seventeen times over by his own confession—and implored Hicksey to settle the business out of hand. "If I'm sent to Rangoon,' said he, 'they'll keep me in jail all my life, and that is a death every time the sun gets up or the wind blows.' But we had to send him to Rangoon; and, of course, he was let off down there and given penal servitude for life. When I came to Rangoon I went over the jail—I had helped to fill it, y' know—and the old Boh was there and recognized me at once. He begged for some opium first, and I tried to get him some; but that was against the rules. Then he asked me to have his sentence changed to death, because he was afraid of being sent to the Andamans. I couldn't do that, either; but I tried to cheer him and told him how the row was going up country. And the last thing he said was: 'Give my compliments to the fat white man who jumped on me. If I'd been awake I'd have killed him.' I wrote to Hicksey next mail, and— that's all. I'm 'fraid I've been gassing awf'ly, sir."

Cleever said nothing for a long time. The Infant looked uncomfortable. He feared that, misled by enthusiasm, he had filled up the novelist's time with unprofitable recital of trivial anecdotes.

Then said Cleever: "I can't understand it. Why should you have seen and done all these things before you have cut your wisdom-teeth?"

"Don't know," said the Infant, apologetically. "I haven't seen much—only Burmese jungle."

"And dead men and war and power and responsibility," said Cleever, under his breath. "You won't have any sensations left at thirty if you go on as you have done. But I want to hear more tales—more tales." He seemed to forget that even subalterns might have engagements of their own.

"We're thinking of dining out somewhere, the lot of us, and going on to the Empire afterward," said Nevin, with hesitation. He did not like to ask Cleever to come too. The invitation might be regarded as "cheek." And Cleever, anxious not to wag a gray beard unbidden among boys at large, said nothing on his side.

Boileau solved the little difficulty by blurting out: "Won't you come too, sir?"

Cleever almost shouted "Yes," and while he was being helped into his coat, continued to murmur "Good heavens!" at intervals, in a manner that the boys could not understand.

"I don't think I've been to the Empire in my life," said he. "But, good heavens! what is my life, after all? Let us go back."

So they went out with Eustace Cleever, and I sulked at home, because the boys had come to see me, but had gone over to the better man, which was humiliating. They packed him into a cab with utmost reverence, for was he not the author of "As it was in the Beginning," and a person in whose company it was an honor to go abroad? From all I gathered later, he had taken no less interest in the performance before him than in the boys' conversation, and they protested with emphasis that he was "as good a man as they make, knew what a man was driving at almost before he said it, and yet he's so dashed simple about things any man knows." That was one of many comments made afterward.

At midnight they returned, announcing that they were highly respectable gondoliers, and that oysters and stout were what they chiefly needed. The eminent novelist was still with them, and I think he was calling them by their shorter names. I am certain that he said he had been moving in worlds not realized, and that they had shown him the Empire in a new light. Still sore at recent neglect, I answered shortly: "Thank Heaven, we have within the land ten thousand as good as they!" and when Cleever departed, asked him what he thought of things generally.

He replied with another quotation, to the effect that though singing was a remarkably fine performance, I was to be quite sure that few lips would be moved to song if they could find a sufficiency of kissing.

Whereat I understood that Eustace Cleever, decorator and color man in words, was blaspheming his own art, and that he would be sorry for this in the morning.

THE END